MY ADVENTURE

IN

THE QUEST OF

DIAMONDS

SALAHUDDIN AYYUBI

(SALAUDDIN)

Contents

CHAPTER 1: START OF MY JOURNEY FOR DIAMONDS.

My name is Ishaan Loknayak. My father Sanjay Loknayak owns a sweet shop in one of the busiest streets of Palghat. It is a small town near the Yamuna River in Utter Pradesh. My mother Pooja Loknayak was only a housewife and I have one sister named Roshni Loknayak, who is five years older than me.

I can distinctly remember that morning, the breeze was serener than usual. It was Sunday still I woke up early in the morning because I had to go outside to a nearby playground for playing cricket with my friends. I was in eighth class and look wise I was slimmer than most of the boys of my age. After playing cricket I came to my home and had breakfast. After that, I went to my father's sweet shop. Sometimes I used to sit at the counter of the shop, my father had already thought that I was only born to sit on the counter of the shop because I was never good at studies since my childhood. I would always get passing marks only.

While I was sitting at the counter of the shop, I first time saw her. In the jewellery shop in front of our shop. Her age was perhaps equal to my age. Although I was not able to listen, what she was saying but the way she was talking to the shop owner of that shop, she was perhaps his daughter. Her face was shining in the sunlight and the shining nose pin on her sharp nose was piercing my heart. I was staring at her and suddenly she glanced toward me. I hesitantly retraced my gaze toward my counter. My father was busy on the other hand attending to customers. After a few seconds I once again glanced toward the jewellery shop, she was saying something to her father and suddenly both of them looked toward our shop and it seemed that she had told her father that I was staring at her. Both she and her father started coming toward our shop. I started dripping on my seat and my forehead was covered in sweat in no time. Soon she and her father were right in front of my counter. She looked at her father and spoke.

"This is the boy, dad."

Her father eyeballed at me and spoke.

"So, you are the boy"

I was perspiring copiously and started stammering and was hardly able to say.

"No, no, I was not …"

The girl chuckled while I was dripping and with blush, she gazed toward her father and said once again.

"Yes dad, this is the boy who was saying that in this shop the best milk cakes are made, I also want to eat some milk cakes."

After saying so she blushed again as if she was intentionally teasing me. And just then she winked at me. I felt much-needed relief. I became instantly dynamic after that as if I had got some kind of instant power surge and said to her father.

"Yes uncle, in our shop we make the best milk cakes in all over Utter Pradesh if you don't believe then you can try it."

I gave two pieces of milk cake, one to the girl and another to the uncle. Both ate the milk cake and they seemed to enjoy it immensely. The sweets in our shop were famous for their taste.

"Yeah, it sure tastes wonderful. All right, pack 2 Kg of this sweet," said the uncle. Both departed our shop and entered their shop, while on the way she again glimpsed at me and blushed.

***

The rest of the day was spent in those dreams like memories of that blush and of course that wink. Was she also interested in me, was the only thought that was mingling in my mind? Soon enough it was dark, and my father proceeded for closing the shop. At home also I was in a dream-like state. Seeing me like that my mother became worried. I was sitting at the dining table and was having dinner, but my mind was completely lost in the memories of that girl.

"Oh, my dear son, what are you thinking? Concentrate on your food." said mother in a loud yet humble tone.

I saw toward the face of my mother in the same dream-like state.

"What happened to you? Did someone say something?" asked my mother now her face was evidently, concerned for me.

It took a few seconds for me to realize my situation and the way I was having my food,

"Nothing mom, nobody has told me anything. I am just feeling sleepy and nothing else. Don't worry mom." I said somehow convincing my mom.

After having dinner, I went straight to my bed.

***

The next day in the school I saw her during the Morning Prayer assembly. She also noticed me and smiled at me. After that, my mind was continuously diverting to her during classes. The recess bell rang, and I went to the sports ground along with my friends. Aditya Rana was my best friend in my class. Most of the time I would hang out with him. He also accompanied me to the playground.

I along with my friends was playing football on the ground. After some time, I noticed that she was standing beside the ground and was looking toward me. I gazed at her then she smiled. My friend Aditya noticed this and came over to me.

"Yo dude, she is looking at you I think she is interested in you. Leave the football and go to her," said Aditya with a mischievous smile on his face.

"I also think so, but I don't dare to approach her. Will you come with me?" I said almost in an imploring manner.

"Yeah sure, after all, I am your friend. I will help you in sailing the ocean of beauty waiting for you to conquer it." After saying so, Aditya blushed.

"All right, now let's go."

While saying so he held my hand started almost dragging me to her. One friend of hers came to her and started a conversation with her. The other girl was also beautiful, but not as beautiful as her.

I along with Aditya went toward her. Seeing me she blushed slightly.

"Hi," I said to her.

"Hi," she replied. "Do you work in a sweet shop? I saw you in that sweet shop which is in front of my father's jewellery shop in the market. My father bought sweets from you, do you remember?"

"Ya, I remember and No," I said, "I don't work there. That is the shop of my father. My family is running the shop for generations."

"Oh, I see," she replied.

"By the way, I am in eighth class in section A, my name is Ishaan Loknayak, and" while pointing toward my friend I said, "he is my classmate and friend Aditya Rana."

She smiledand said,

"Nice to meet you, Ishaan, my name is Anya Singhania," while looking at her friend she further said, "She is my friend, her name is Prachi Deshmukh."

After that we talked about a few normal things like the school environment, aims of life, about our shops, etc. Aditya and Prachi were already acquaintances to each other, as they both, had home in the same street near my home in Palghat.

After that day we usually met in school after recess and all four of us became quite good friends. Anya was very fond of jewellery. She used to wear different types of earrings and nose rings every day. All those pieces of jewellery seemed quite expensive.

Similarly, many days passed, years passed, and we passed secondary school and after that senior secondary school. I got admission to B.A. with psychology, and she got admission to B.Sc. with physics as a subject. Although our college was the same, it was named District College of higher Studies.

***

I had a bike by then and I used to pick Anya while going to college. Everything was perfect. We used to go for outings on Sundays and College together and sometimes to movies. I liked her but I did not dare to say her.

One day I was having lunch in the college canteen along with Anya. It was sweet and partly cloudy summer weather. She was looking stunning as usual in her light pink frock. Her loose hair on her forehead was dwindling with the breeze. We were having pasta during lunch. While taking a spoonful of pasta and sliding her dwindling hair over her ear, she gazed at me and said,

"Well, Ishaan, have you thought about what you want to become in your life? You know everyone here during graduation is thinking about their career and you must also,"

"Nothing much, just the same family business I am supposed to take over from my dad, I mean sweet shop business. And what about you, what are you planning to do? Are you also planning to take over your father's business?" I asked her while gazing at her face.

"Nah, I won't take over my father's business, my brother might do that," she said and stopped momentarily as if she was thinking something seriously and gripped herself into it and once again she vocalised while frowning and squinting,

"I don't like studies, it's so boring. Only rote memorization is done in college nowadays and that is not my cup of tea, I hate it," she said while expanding the hate word for a few seconds.

"So, what is your plan, Anya?" I asked, looking at her beautiful thoughtful face which was becoming more gorgeous when she was thinking hard.

"Nothing special, just no to studies after graduation. I want to marry a wealthy guy when my graduation is over, he might be from a business class family or jewellery family or any other big business family," she replied with enthusiasm on her face while saying so.

"So, you like your future husband to be a businessman, by the way, if you don't mind can I ask which business you prefer the most," I asked while in fear of seeing the end of my one-sided love life in front of me. Although I have liked her for so long, yet I was not able to tell her my feelings and now she was telling this thing that she would marry some wealthy guy. Although my family owned a sweet shop for generations, yet we were only a middle-class family. The reason for this somewhat goes to the honesty approach of my father. He never adulterated any of the sweet being sold in the shop. Many a time my mother also used to say that other sweet selling families have become so rich selling sweets made by adulterated material and used to ask why my father was not doing so. And my father always used to say that "honesty is the best policy, Whatever a man faces in his life he must never forget this policy."

She finished her pasta and drank water from the bottle, the bottle which she always refused to share with anyone.

"I," while lengthening the pronunciation of it she replied "want to get married to a diamond business owner. I like diamonds seriously."

I had also finished my pasta until now. While looking at her face I said, "so you like diamonds that much?"

"Yeah, no kidding." She replied while blushing and of course talking about jewellery especially diamonds was one of her hobbies.

"So," I said, "if you happened to meet a guy, I mean a good-looking guy like me and if he has a diamond business then will you marry him?"

"Yeah sure," she smiled again and winked at me, "why any other guy if you somehow manage to open a diamond business, I will think about marrying you. Don't underestimate yourself. You are quite handsome indeed."

At that point, I felt that she might be interested in me genuinely if I had a diamond business. It was only the status of my family and her family that was becoming the impediment between us. Although, many people say that true love does not bother about money. But in practical life, money has its place. She belonged to a business class family, and it was sure that her father would never marry her to any middle-class guy like me. It was at that point of time when I decided that I will deviate from my family-owned business of the sweet shop, and I would indulge in the diamond business.

"All right," I said while looking at her, as she was playing with a part of fringe falling over her right eye,

"if I start my own diamond business then you might accept me also as your husband?"

She giggled listening to this and said,

"I knew that you have an eye on me," she blushed a bit. While stammering I said,

"No, it is not like that. I was just asking you kiddingly."

"Oh please," she said while making a hand gesture as if she is slapping an invisible face in the air.

"I always had an intuition that you liked me so don't hide it. By the way, I also like you, but your status does not match the status of my family. I know that you would say, in love status does not matter and blah blah blah. But you should understand, in marriage, status does matter. And even I don't want to feel humiliated after marrying some sweet shop owner, please don't mind,"

Although She was speaking whatever was in her mind and I was getting her point, still I was feeling somewhat hurt. It was easy for her to say don't mind but those words fell sharply through my ear.

"Yeah, I can understand," I said while deviating my gaze to the blue and partly clouded sky and once again looked at her,

"Don't worry. I, sometimes think that I should raise my status. After all, until how long I will do the same old family business. I should make a new path for myself and now I am thinking about doing business in diamond dealings." I said.

"Oho, so that you can propose to me. Is that so?" she blushed.

"No that is not the case. Although, if I become successful in my endeavour I might think about it," I said with a chuckle and while gazing at her.

"Oh!" was her only response with a giggle.

After that, we went to our classes.

***

After college, I met my friend Aditya in his room. His home was almost within walking distance of my home. He was watching a movie in his room. It was the time of evening.

"So, what's going these days?" I enquired while sitting on one of the chairs in his room. On another chair, he was sitting and watching a movie on a laptop. The laptop was placed on a small study table. There was a small bed beside one of the walls behind my chair.

"Nothing special, just watching movies and preparing for the final semester exam, you say what's going on these days? Did you make any progress with Anya?" Aditya asked.

"Same here just preparing for the final semester exam and after the exam, I will have to involve in the family business. But I do not want to get involved in the sweet selling shop. I want to do something big in my life. And about Anya, yeah finally she said that she likes me, but she does not like the profession of my family," I replied to Aditya.

He gazed toward me in haste, away from the screen of the laptop, on which the action sequence of some Hollywood movie was being played in full swing with a loud musical sound. He lowered the sound of the movie and said contemplatively.

"If she likes you then what is the problem? And about your shop. I must say that running a sweet shop is a very decent business, why does she not like your family business?"

"She is saying that she may like me if I do some big business, like a business of diamond? I too don't want to sit in a sweet shop. The diamond business is a good idea. What do you say about it?" I asked Aditya.

Considering for a while what I had just said, Aditya gazed at me and said.

"Diamond business is a very tough one, I think. It will require a lot of capital and tell me, bro, how you will get that, have you thought about it?"

"I will think about it, first of all, I think I need to do some marketing research about how to start a diamond business?" I said.

"Yeah, that is a nice idea, by the way, I have heard about a new diamond trading company. It was founded by a young entrepreneur last year only. I think his name is Rocky Bhati. Within a year, his company has made a name amongst the top ten diamond companies in the world and, wealth wises he is amongst top 200 wealthy Indian," he replied.

"What is the name of his company anyway, we can meet him or do an internship in his company to get some idea about how diamond business is done. What do you say?" I asked.

"Let me search on google. I am not recollecting the name of his company. Wait a minute," he replied and opened google on his laptop. In a few minutes, he searched everything about Rocky Bhati.

On the Wikipedia page. Everything was written about him. Rocky Bhati was rather a young man of about thirty-year age. Look wise, he was neither slim nor obese, yet he was muscular. He had a small and sharp moustache. He had opened his diamond business company last year only. The name of his company was 'Sparkling Diamond Pvt. Ltd.'. Within one year it has become one of the famous diamond companies in the world. It had net revenue of 10000 crores in one year of its business in one year only.

I and Aditya decided that when we would finish our final semester exam then we would go to this company to know about the diamond business and if

Rocky Bhati would not be interested in telling us how he managed to grow his company so fast within one year. We would try to join his company as an intern. And hence my journey for diamonds started there. At that time, I would have never thought in the wildest of my dream what mysterious incidents would happen to me. Everything which I could say that can only occur in the dream or some fantasy movie was going to happen with me. My life was about to take a bizarre and roller coaster turn befitting a Hollywood movie.

CHAPTER 2: A KIND-HEARTED

HERO

I somehow cleared the final semester exam of graduation. After that, I thought about pursuing my goal. First, I had to talk with my father about this.

It was Sunday. It was the month of July, and it was raining profoundly outside. So, my father had decided against opening the shop. It was around 11 a.m. and he was sitting in the living room and watching the news on TV. I also went there and sat on one of the sofas beside him.

"What's going on these days, son," asked my father.

"Nothing special. Just passed graduation so I am thinking about doing something, I think some business is a good idea, what do you say, dad" I asked.

Listening to this my father became puzzled and looked toward me with his piercing gaze and said.

"What! Do you want to start a business? We already have a sweet shop business, and you are my only son. It is you who will manage the shop. Don't think about any other business." My father replied in a somewhat rude tone.

"But dad," I said "I don't want to sit on the sweet shop I want to do some big business. I want to start a diamond business."

"Oho so my dear son wants to do diamond business" he replied almost like taunting me "so from where you will get so much money?"

"I know you have fixed deposits in the bank" I replied, "you can give me that money and when my business will be well established, I will return your money."

"What are you thinking, son," my father yelled "is doing business a child's play? Many people became bankrupt in trying a new business. You already have your well-established family business. Why do you want to venture into a new business? That too, a business of diamonds. Do you have any experience or knowledge about that?"

"I will get knowledge and experience. I will contact Rocky Bhati. He is an emerging businessman in the field of the diamond business." I replied "after getting an idea from him how to do business in diamonds. I will establish my own company."

"And you think he will tell you his secret with all eagerness," said my father while smirking a bit, "my dear son no one will tell you his business secrets. Forget about it. You will have to discover business secrets by yourself. And suppose somehow you get an idea about diamond business; I know he will not tell you by himself. You will have to work in his company for it. And if you work in his company and somehow get an idea still forget that I will give you money for your new adventure. Don't forget you have one elder sister. I will have to get her married, and I am saving money for that only. So don't bring ever in front of me this nonsense talk of starting a new business of diamonds. You will not be able to start this business. There is a lot of competition in the market and about financing, It is very tough nowadays."

"But father," I said, "let me try at least once, if I fail, I will join in our family business of selling sweets in a tiny shop."

"All right son, I give you one whole year so that you can prove yourself. And if after even one year you are not able to start your diamond business then you will have to work in our shop only and forget about your business ideas," my father said to me in a stern reprimanding voice.

"Father what can I do in only one year," I asked father, "you are not even giving me money. I will have to finance my business myself. First, I will have to learn all strategies then I will require finance. All of this will take at least three years."

"So, you are asking for three years," said my father.

"Yes father, I require at least three years", I replied.

"All right, I give you three years. If you did not become successful in your diamond adventure after that, then you will have to do our family business, did you get it?" said my father.

"Then father, you will see, after three years I will be the best businessman of diamonds in this country," I said in excitement.

"We shall see," replied my father.

***

I along with my friend Aditya started making plans to start our diamonds company. We decided that we would be a 50 per cent partnership each in the company. The name of our company would be Epic Diamonds private limited. After thinking about all of this we tried many times to get an appointment with Rocky Bhati, but we were not successful. After trying many times in vain, we decide to join the same company. We gave interviews with the company for any position available. There were two positions available for the packaging of diamonds at the mine area of diamonds. The company had its mine area in goa. We were posted there.

I along with Aditya took our posting letters and headed for goa. The mine was in a deserted plane. It was surrounded by highly raised walls. Near the entry gate of mines was the office where all the packaging work was done and in the same building, the living rooms for workers were given. In the ground and first-floor packaging, quality control and distribution were done. Beyond the first floor, there were three more floors. The second floor was for the manager of the mine. The third and fourth floor was given to the workers for lodgings. I and Aditya were given a single room on the fourth floor. It was a simple small room having two separate beds. The kitchen and bathrooms were attached inside. There was a small balcony available which was on the front side of the building. From the balcony, the high and mighty gate of the mine was visible. For packaging, there was only one other guy other than us. In total there were about only 10 employees in this mine. For being a mine, this was a very little number of employees. I tried to ask on my first day to other guys working in the mine, but they were also unaware of the reason why there are so few people working in this mine, although this mine generates 10000 crore turnovers in one year. The wall surrounding the mine was very highly raised it was even higher than the building in which the packaging work was done, and we lived. Within a few days, we learnt all the packaging work.

One of the nights in that building. I and Aditya returned to our room after finishing the day's work. Although work was not that extreme, yet our salary was somewhat decent. Aditya and I were given 40000 per month. We had our dinner in the common mess and then returned to our room for getting a rest.

"It has been five months, but we have not gained any knowledge," I said sulking about not being able to learn any useful stuff.

"Yeah, it has been five months away from home and the manager does not give vacations as well. By the way, I have learnt somewhat, how to examine whether a diamond is original or fake. I think this will be helpful in our business when we'll start it." Replied Aditya.

"I also have now some idea about the purity of diamonds. But we must learn how the diamond is mined. I don't know why the manager does not allow us to enter into the mine, we could learn their process of mining. Here we only see diamonds and Categorize them according to their quality and pack. That's all" I replied in a complaining tone.

"Don't be dismayed bro," replied Aditya trying to soothe me, "whatever we are learning here will surely help us in our business. Have patience buddy. Starting one's own business requires a great amount of learning and patience. And to recognize diamonds and categorize them according to their purity is also an art. We will surely get benefitted by it."

"You are right, but I am eager to go inside the mine. When will we go inside? Only the manager goes inside along with Vijay, Ashok, and Tinku in the truck to fetch diamonds from the mine. I think they are very trusted to the manager. We should also talk to the manager that we also want to go inside the mine. We also wanted to be more prolific to the company" I said to Aditya.

"Hmm," said Aditya "I don't know why the manager doesn't allow us to go inside mine. We have spent almost five-month here. We have done our work faithfully. I think it's a matter of diamond that's why only a few trusted people are allowed to go inside the mine. I have asked the manager many times about going inside the mine, but he always denies it. I think you should also ask the manager."

"Yeah, I will surely ask the manager, he should allow us inside the mine. After all, it has been 5 months working here why he does not trust us", I said with full confidence that the other day I would surely ask the manager about it.

***

The next day, it was almost 11 am. I was busy categorizing diamonds according to their qualities. It was a sampling hall on the ground floor. Adjacent to it was the packaging hall. Within one month I and Aditya had been upgraded from packager of diamonds to the sampler of diamonds according to their quality.

"How's sampling going, you work very hard boys," was the voice of the manager. The manager was a short guy with a dense moustache on his face. On his right cheek, there was a distinct black wart that was giving him the look of a Bollywood villain of 80s movies.

"Yeah, it's going perfectly all right. I have learnt it very well. Although I was never good at studies, I feel that my natural talent rests in knowing the exact quality of diamonds and sorting them according to that quality." I replied to the manager.

"That's nice. I can see you are working very hard. You will soon go very high in this company I am sure about It.," said the manager. Aditya was also sorting diamonds at another table. The manager looked at him and stated.

"You also, in fact, both of you will reach a much higher position in this company. Just keep on doing your work with the same honesty and zeal."

"Sure sir, we will do," we both replied.

"Ok then I am going to my office, you guys carry on," said the manager while started strolling outside the hall.

"Sir," I said. He stopped and looked at me.

"Yes boy, say."

"Sir, I want to say that it has been over five months since we are working here. Still, we have not gone inside the mine. If you don't mind. Can we go inside?" I said to the manager in a firm and decisive tone.

"Yeah, sure," the manager said, "Rocky sir has just laid down a policy that whichever employee will do his work with utmost honesty for five years will have a chance to go inside the mine. And, whatever amount of diamond he collects there, 1 per cent of the income from that diamond will belong to that employee. So be happy just continue your good work for five years then you will be able to go inside the mine."

"But sir," I said, "five years is a very long time, don't you think"?

"Yeah, it is," replied the manager "but it's worth the reward you will get after five years."

"Yes, sir. I understand," I replied. Although I was apparently calm but deep inside, I was furious.

"That's like a good boy. You understand things so easily, keep it up," said the manager and went to his office. And we continued our work there.

***

At night we again were in our room. I was a little impatient by then. I was lounging on my bed and Aditya was idling on his bed after having dinner.

"Bro, the manager is saying that it will take five years to go there. I cannot wait that long" I said to Aditya.

"But what we can do about it," replied Aditya worryingly. "I think we will have to leave this company now and try some other company where they allow us to go inside the mine. After all, we have gained enough experience in checking the quality of diamonds here."

"No, that will take time," I said to Aditya, "whether the manager allows it or not I will certainly go tomorrow inside the mine, are you coming with me or not," I said with firm intention to visit the mine from inside.

"But how we will go inside?" asked Aditya.

"That's very simple," I replied "The manager uses a numeric password to open the gate of mine, and a few days ago I had made a video of him on my phone while he was entering the password. I had thought that I will use it as a last resort if the manager deny us entry."

"Oh, so you have… the password of the gate," replied Aditya in amazement.

"Yep, I have the password and tomorrow evening we will go inside the mine, all right," I said with confidence.

"What if we get caught? The manager may turn us over to police," replied Aditya in apprehension.

"Don't worry bro," I said while reassuring him, "we will go inside and see all around. And we will try to figure out how diamonds are mined there. Then we will return as soon as possible. Just chill out nothing will happen."

"Then it's all right," he said. Afterwards, we talked for a few more minutes, and then we both drove off to sleep. During sleep, I had a very strange dream. In that dream, I was falling toward darkness. There were only brick walls I could see all around me. Very far above me, I was able to see Aditya. Above him, the light was being illuminated such that his face was not visible clearly. I was falling in darkness and Aditya was becoming small and small as the farther I went downward in darkness. Just then my downward freefall stopped momentarily, and I started being pulled toward the light, in the direction where Aditya was standing and looking toward me. Slowly and slowly Aditya was coming toward me. And then something strange happened, the light behind Aditya that was illuminating Aditya from behind, increased its brightness for a few seconds. I was not able to see Aditya clearly for a few seconds. When the intensity of light became normal again then once again, I glanced toward Aditya, but what I was seeing, was not Aditya; a girl was standing in the place of Aditya. I was being hauled toward that girl. She seemed around 25 years old and was very fair. She had sharp facial features and small lips. Her eyes were big and glistening. She was wearing a white suit and a salwar.

I was continuously being pulled toward her. A few seconds later I was almost in the position of collision with her but just then I became still in the air. She was also floating beside me. The darkness beneath me was vanishing and brick laid road appeared there. She held me in her lap, and she gently touched the ground. All around me, old country-styled houses appeared, and those houses were not visible clearly. As they were partially visible in the white fog.

She slowly let me off from her lap and I gently alighted myself to the ground. She alighted herself to the ground. She was looking very strained and said.

"Kind-hearted sir," a few drops of tears appeared over her cheek. "Only you can save us. I am begging you please save us from a curse that has overshadowed our kingdom. Legend says that only a person of pure heart can save us from this darkness of mind and soul."

Just after she had finished her statement. The fog all around us which was of slightly white colure changed its colour into dark black. She becomes very anxious and gasped for a few seconds.

"Now, please come to us by the well, not tomorrow but today. You can only come to us today, tomorrow it will be very late for us, please kind-hearted sir, and please save us."

Everything disappeared in front of me, and I was awakened from my dream. I was breathing profoundly. I awakened Aditya and told him about my dream.

"It was just a dream bro, go to sleep, it is 3 am," said Aditya while looking at the watch and while still in a dreamlike state. "We will go tomorrow inside the mine; I mean today evening. Let me sleep bro," he insisted. I also thought that it is just a dream, and I will go in the evening. I lied down for having sleep, Again.

Once again, I went into another dream. This time I was in a lush green jungle. Very high trees were all around me. I looked all around. The same white fog was present all around. And again, that white fog turned into black mist. This time a man appeared in front of me. He was wearing a black clock in such a way that his face was not visible. The nails of his hand were very big; I thought he had not cut them for years. He was looking wicked.

"So, you are the crusader of these pathetic people. I can see very dim life energy in you. How will you fight with me, you, meek dork? Tell me why you have opted to become their prophet, ha, ha, ha, although you seem so coward," his voice was very deep and harsh.

"I did not understand what you are saying, sir. I think I am having a dream and you are just a character of my dream," I said while stuttering in front of him. His voice was extremely frightening such that any sane person will grovel in front of him. He laughed once again.

"Ha, ha, ha, so you are thinking that this is a dream," then he smirked a bit, "what a pity."

As his face was covered by the clock so I was not able to see clearly. "Very well then," he held his hand in front of his chest as if he was holding something in his hand. Just then a sword appeared in his hand. It was a shimmering sword made of pure diamond. It was the highest quality diamond. I had done so much sampling that I could recognize simply by seeing the quality of any diamonds. Then he said,

"If it is a dream as you acclaim, then if I cut your head with my sword then you will surely not die, I think," he said in his usual harsh and rough voice. I was having doubts by then because it was all feeling extremely real.

Although I knew that I had gone to sleep a while ago, but I had never had a dream so vivid. Everything was looking so real.

"I think whether I am dreaming or not. Getting decapitated is not a good idea," I stuttered once again. He laughed and said.

"Such a meek man you are. You are not worth living," and after saying so he swung his blade toward my throat. Before the sword could hit my throat, I was wrapped up by a shining rope and was pulled instantly backwards. She was the same girl in the white dress of my dream before this dream. She put her hand above her head and white light emanated from her hand everything got illuminated.

Once again, I woke up from the dream. This time that beautiful girl was in my room. She was gasping for air. While breathing heavily she said,

"I have used all of my power. Now I can't save you further in this realm. Please enter our realm. The only way through which you can enter our realm is the passage of well. Go inside the passage of well in this mine. Please come to our realm and save all of us. Within a few hours, the pathway to our realm will be closed forever, and if you did not come to save us then we all will perish. Please kind-hearted hero. Save us." She was sobbing, and tears were emanating from her eyes continuously. Just then she became a little translucent and then transparent and then she disappeared completely. Aditya was snoring on his bed.

CHAPTER 3: THE WELL OF

DIAMONDS

I awakened Aditya and told him what had happened just a while ago with

me. For some time, he stared at me frustratingly in utter disbelief then he muttered in half-sleep.

"How can this happen? How can anyone come out of a dream?" he said.

"I don't know," I told him while in an utterly perplexed state myself,

"I know all these things seem improbable but," I stopped for a while and had a few deep breaths, "but the way she was sobbing and suddenly disappeared, and there was that dreadful man in the black cloak and why he attacked me with a sword. I have so many questions. I don't feel that this is just a dream."

"Bro," he said with an annoyed look, "you just had a bad dream, just forget about it. I think you are planning to go inside the mine and cheat on this company that's why you are having such bad dreams. Now please sleep and let me also sleep in peace." He had become frustrated with me as this was the second time I had awakened him.

I remained seated for a few minutes on my bed. The way that beautiful girl was sobbing, all seemed real to me.

"Very well," I said to Aditya "if you do not want to go there, I, myself, will go there in the mine and see what this matter is about the well, about which the lady in my dream was talking again and again."

"Please bro, don't be so adamant. Let me sleep and you should also sleep now." Said Aditya.

"Fine," I stood up from my bed changed the clothes and then started to go outside. I opened the gate of my room and went outside. I shut the gate behind me. Walked toward the lift. I entered the lift and pushed the button for the ground floor. The gates of the lift were in the process of closing. Just then a hand appeared between the gates. The gate opened once again. Aditya entered the lift. I saw him and chuckled. He was looking a little frustrated.

"What the hell you are thinking. Now you have started chasing dreams," he said to me in a complaining tone. I looked at his face. I pressed again the button for the ground floor.

"It was so vivid dream Aditya. Try to understand," I said.

"All right let's investigate your dream, and if it just came to be a dream then we will not go into that mine ever again," he said.

"Ok, bro, sure," I said.

He glanced at me, and he waggled his head left and right two or three times while having a deep sigh.

After a few seconds, we were on the ground floor. We came out of the lift. The main gate was guarded by a guard, but he was fast asleep. I had never seen him sleeping at that time. I was having some menacing thought that someone might have been helping me for his evil intention so that I can go inside the mine easily. I went outside the main gate of the building and started strolling quietly toward the main gate of the mine. The light tower beside the main gate was manned by two guards. They were also seemed to be fast asleep. Aditya was also following me. While slowly going toward the main gate I asked Aditya in a faint voice,

"Don't you feel it a little strange?".

"Yeah, absolutely it is quite strange. It is about 3 am in the night and we are walking like nocturnal species here, surely it is strange," he mocked me.

"No, dude" I replied while looking all around attentively, "I am not saying about that, I am saying about guards, they all are sleeping. What do you think maybe the reason? Around this time, they usually remain alert. Could it be possible that someone is helping us? Your thought about it?"

"I don't know buddy," while yawning he said, "I only know that I have to get more sleep, let's make it haste to examine your so-called well told by a lady appeared in your dream and located inside the mine and after satisfying yourself that you had only dreamed about it. We will return as soon as possible to complete my much-needed sleep."

"Ok," I mumbled, "Just don't say this loudly."

Both of us reached the main gate of the mine. I entered the password which I had already video graphed on my phone when the manager was entering it one day. The gate of mine opened. We entered inside the mine and the gate closed behind us. It was very dark inside. We switched on the flashlights of our phones. There was a bitumen road in front of us. The width of the road was about 15 feet. On both sides of the road, it was like a deserted place. Trees were completely dried and were also in very little quantity. There was much darkness inside the mine than outside the mine.

"It seems like some haunted place, I am getting frightened," said Aditya while looking all around.

"Don't get frightened," I said to Aditya, "let's go ahead and investigate about this mine."

We walked further along the road. For a few minutes it seemed like a deserted road there was nothing on both sides except a few dried-up ancient worldly trees and dried up portions of the trunks of the trees. After a few more minutes we saw a ruin of a house. It was beside the road and looked like a hotel. It had 3 stories and was spread in about 5000 square feet.

"What this ruin of building doing in this mine, it's quite strange. Do diamonds come from this ruined building," said Aditya. He was visibly puzzled seeing a ruined house inside the mine. I was also curious to see it.

"Yeah, it's quite strange. Let's go further and see what other strange things we find here; I now feel why the manager was not allowing us to enter this mine there is something strange going on behind those highly raised walls of it," I said but my mind was pondering further about the strangeness of things appearing inside the mine.

We moved further along the road. Few more ruined houses appeared on both sides of the road. The white mist appeared as we moved ahead on the road giving haunted look to everything all around and due to mist visibility became quite low. After walking for a while on the same road and looking at all those ruins in a perplexed mode we reached a junction where the road parted in three ways. There were boards beside each way. Those boards were in dilapidated conditions as if they had been erected decades ago, over one of the boards a blackbird, almost the same as that of crow was sitting, it had an almost parrot-like beak. We were frightened seeing that junction but somehow regained strength and read those boards. On the right one, it was written community hall, on the left one it was written, primary school, and on the board on the straight road ahead on it was written, community well. Seeing this Aditya looked to me.

"Can this be the well of your dream?" Aditya asked strangely but inside he might have been thinking that well must not be found so that he could complete his sleep.

"I don't know, let's see what this is," I replied.

"Yeah, sure," he yawned.

We both moved toward the middle path. On this path also various ruins of buildings were visible in slight white mist. After a few minutes, there was a ruin of a small school. It was a front side very wide wall and a small gate in the middle of the wall. Behind the gate, there was a small vacant area and behind that the ruin of the building was, it was hardly visible, it was in extremely dilapidated condition.

We moved further, after a few minutes, as we were walking taking small and careful steps, a small piece of diamond came flying toward us and fell near our feet. I held the diamond and started examining it, it was an average quality diamond. A few minutes later one more diamond came hurtling toward us, I examined it also, it was high-quality diamonds. Diamonds were coming from the right side and the road was also divided there, one going straight and the other taking a sharp right turn at a 90-degree angle. We turned to the right. The white mist on that road was denser than the mist we had seen so far. Using the flashlight of phones, we somehow crawled forward slowly. Within a few feet ahead I was able to see the caricature of a well faintly amidst the white mist. We went toward the well. It was extremely putrefied. It was made of red bricks and black and green algae were visible on it. As we were staring at this ugly well Aditya said,

"Is this the well about which the girl in your dream was saying?"

"I don't know let me check inside of it," I replied.

I went near the well and peeped into it. It was stark dark beneath. Just then two diamonds hurled out from the well and fell nearby. We were gawkily looking at each other.

"Holy god! What is this? Diamond expelling well. I can't believe it," said Aditya in shock. It was just an unbelievable event for us to see.

"That's why that manager was not allowing us to enter into the mine. It was almost like a diamond fountain we are seeing here. That's why there are so few employees on this site. They don't have to mine diamonds, it is just freely available here." I said while picking one of the diamonds collapsed there.

As I was talking a few more diamond pieces of varying quality came out of the well as if someone was deliberately throwing them out of it.

"So, this is the case with diamond mining here. But if a diamond comes out so freely from this well how this information is valuable for us in establishing our future diamond company. I mean there is no real mine here. It is pure luck of rocky that he discovered this well and this ruined town." Aditya said. He was hopeless now as we had not found any useful information.

"And also," I replied to Aditya, "he doesn't want that his secret be exposed by anyone that's why he built so high raised wall all around the mine and the ruined well, I now understood so phenomenal rise in fortune of rocky. It was only luck and pure luck nothing else."

"Yeah, I also think so. But what we will do for our business?" pondered Aditya.

"First of all," I said, "I will make video graphed evidence of all this and expose rocky in front of everyone."

I opened the camera on my mobile and started video graphing everything. The outpouring of diamonds from the well and the ruin all around it. I was standing extremely close to the wall of the well. Just then few beams of light hit on my face and the face of Aditya. I put my palm in front of my face.

"What are you guys doing here?" it was the voice of the manager. "You boys have seen too much and after that, we can not take any risk. Both of you can reveal our secret to government agencies and they will confiscate this mine so both of you don't have the right to live now." Then he looked toward Vijay, one of his trusted employees who was also accompanying him. He had a shotgun with him.

"Kill both. They have done the last mistake of their life and this mistake is unredeemable." Then the manager looked to me and Aditya and said,

"You both had lots of potential in you but, alas! Your greed has brought you in this position and this position is the position of demise, this is the end of the line for both of you," then he glanced to Vijay again and yelled, "what are you waiting for, just fire the bullet and kill both of them. If Rocky came to know about this incident then he will surely kill us. So, hide their bodies after killing them,"

Vijay inserted bullets in shotgun and aimed toward Aditya. While aiming at Aditya he grinned in the ugliest possible way. Aditya was trembling in fear. He was becoming hopeless, and the fact was that I was also becoming hopeless. It seemed the end of my life, as I was able to see, by one of the bullets of the gun in the hand of Vijay. Vijay pulled the trigger but just before he could do that Aditya jumped inside the well. And the bullet collided with one of the ruined walls behind the well. The manager looked to Vijay and shouted.

"Stop for a moment don't waste your other bullet on this useless creature," and he saw toward me and shouted once again.

"You can also jump in the well, it might be the less painful way of death otherwise by bullet wound you might quiver painfully for a few hours."

I was standing trembling there with fear and with darkness to my future and in fact with the end of my future. I looked inside the well and thought it might be a good idea to jump there. The bullet wound will be difficult to bear. After thinking about such things for a while, I jumped inside the well while closing my eyes and hoping that some kind of angle would wake me in hell or

heaven, either one of it, I was prepared to land there.

CHAPTER 4: A STRANGE WORLD

I lingered my eyes closed for some time but nothing happened, it seemed I was falling for a while. I opened my eyes. I was falling into darkness. I gazed in the direction of descent and it was downright darkness. I turned my gaze above. The flashlights through the opening of the well were fading away as I was falling toward the darkness. I was falling for quite a time; I was wondering when I would hit the bottom surface or water or whatever that might be. But I did not collide with anything. The light which I was seeing above me from the opening of the well was turning dim and dimmer as time passed and it perished finally. I had fallen very below the surface I thought. The light was visible from below now to the direction in which I was falling. The light started as a mere point and its intensity grew slowly and steadily. Now I was able to see, it was opening of the well beneath me. That was a strange thing for me, as I fell from one opening of the well and now, I was falling toward another opening of the well. In a few seconds, I flew out of the second opening of the well and fell on evenly cut grass outside. It was a garden. I stood up and looked all around. It was day now. A few minutes ago, I was able to clearly remember that it was night. Now then, it was daytime. I looked at the sky, people were flying as if they all have become superman. There was a huge building of glittering glasses in front of the well, between the well and the building lounged the garden area and the well was situated at the centre of the garden at the junction of four pedestrian paths. Few ladies and gentlemen were standing there all around the well. They were talking to each other while looking at me. They seemed bewildered seeing me coming out of the well. It felt like a dream world straight out of some fairy tale. The sun was shining in the sky, but I was not feeling the exasperating warmth, but it was a gentle warmth. One of the ladies came near to me and started telling me something in her language. The language was strange for me. I was not able to understand a thing, what she was saying. She had worn an elegant dress, just like some princess of our world. She seemed of age around 23. Her height was almost equal to mine, or perhaps it was due to those high heel sandals she was wearing, so it became clear that ladies of all places whether normal or fairy one wear high heel sandals. A man also came toward us and now she was talking to him. They were, I think, arguing about something. The man went again to somewhere and the lady was still standing there smiling at me. I also reciprocated with a smile. A few moments later the man came back, and he was holding a device, like a wireless earphone. He gave this device to me and in sign language told me to put it in my ear. After putting the device in my ear, I looked at the lady again, she smiled and said,

"Hello, can you understand me now? What am I saying?"

I saw her smiling face. Her hair was elegantly designed over her head, her temple was a little broad. The jaw was pointy and lips were small and a pointy nose she had. She was more beautiful than many of the Bollywood actresses. I smiled in reciprocation to her and said,

"Yes ma'am, I can now understand you, a while ago I was not able to understand. Is this device responsible for this," I was wondering about the existence of such a device. I thought if such a device existed in my world then no one will have to learn other languages yet they would be able to converse with each other effortlessly.

"Yes, it is a universal language translator. By using this we can understand and say any language of the whole universe, even the language of other realms like yours, and by the way, I welcome you into our realm," she said this while smiling gorgeously.

"I did not understand what you are saying, is this not my world?" I asked while in great wonder seeing the things which were all around me. People were flying. The building was in the sky. As if they were floating. It was apparently like a fairy world. She once again smiled and gazed at me.

"I will answer all your questions, but first we should go to Head Quarter and meet our chief, lady Millicent Cooper, she is the head of Defence department of our Kingdom, and she is the one who saved you from that black-cloaked evil man, while doing so she lost most of her life energy and she is bedridden now."

I was listening to whatever words she spoke in surprise and I said,

"So that beautiful lady who came into my dream was chief of the defence department."

"Yep, the chief of the defence department," she replied and blushed a bit, and she further said, "I am a first ranking officer of the same department, and my name is Hanna Tucker," and while she was indicating toward the man, who was also in his twenties perhaps, she further said, "His name is Aiden Cox and he is my assistance."

"Sir," Aiden cox looked toward me and bent his head a little lower in the position of greeting while closing both of his eyes.

"So," I asked, "Miss Hanna, you are a first ranking officer of the Defence Department."

"Yes," She replied, "it requires extreme luck to become a first-class officer, any person must be able to control at least two forces of nature to become the first-class officer."

"Pardon," I said "forces of nature? I did not understand."

"We will tell you everything first come with us to headquarter, Millicent ma'am must be quite eager to meet you, she had already said that you have crossed to our realm, so we came here to bring you to her," said Hanna Tucker.

"All right," I said.

Both started ascending above the ground. I was staring at them baffled by their sudden stunt of floating above the ground.

"What are you waiting for? Come on, fly, we have to go to headquarter," she said with the same evergreen smile that was on her face.

"I don't know how to fly," I said.

She came back to the ground and came near me. Aiden Cox also came back to the ground.

"Use your life energy to control gravity, and hence you will decrease gravitational attraction between you and earth and thus you would be able to fly.

Everyone can control gravity. So, you can also." She told me.

"So, everyone can control gravity...? I did not get it?"

At this, Aiden Cox replied enthusiastically as if he was eager to impress me or Hanna with his knowledge,

"Sir, there are forces of nature, and people here are categorized according to the number of forces they can control using their life energy. Everyone can control gravitational force. So everyone comes under the first-level citizen, the person who can control electric force also along with gravitational force comes under second-level citizen, and the person who can control gravitational force, electric force, and magnetic force comes under level three citizen, and if a person can also control weak nuclear forces he comes under fourth level citizen, and further, there exists a secret force, which levels the fifth citizen only can control, and after that force comes the greatest force of nature the time force, which can be controlled by god only, no mere mortal or citizen can control it, although various power lusted people tried to control it they all perished."

"Yes, that's all about categories of the citizen, here in this realm," said Hanna Tucker while shifting her gaze from Aiden to me, "I can control electric force as well along with the gravitational force that's why I was able to become first ranking officer of the defence department. Aiden Cox can only control gravitational force, so he is a first-level citizen, and I am a second level citizen."

"All right," I said, "how will it be known which level citizen I am"?

"The testing sphere is in headquarter, you will have to touch that sphere and the testing sphere will tell you your level," she replied.

"But I don't know how to use gravitational force, can you teach me?" I asked.

"It is very easy, just think about space-time curve-all around you, feel its presence and glide yourself over it using the hypothetical construct made by your life energy, that's it, very simple" she replied.

"That may be simple for people of this realm but for me it is impossible. After all, I have come the first time here. How can I use techniques of your realm the very first time," I said while showing little frustration.

"All right, don't be upset, you will soon learn everything," she replied to me, then she offered her hand toward me and said, "hold my hand and I will guide you to headquarter."

"Are you sure?" I asked.

"Don't worry, just hold my hand," she smiled, "I will not forsake your hand, don't worry."

I held her hand. Now I was floating in the air along with her. Aiden cox was also flying just behind us. She was taking me towards clouds in the sky.

As I was flying towards the clouds. Up to some height, other people were flying and going to their destinations. After that height flying vehicles of the shape of cars appeared and they were flying inside cylindrical airways, made of transparent glass-like surfaces, they were flying with extreme speed,

"So, people from here use flying cars as well although they can fly themselves," I asked Hanna Tucker.

"For small distance, we can fly, but for the large distances we prefer flying cars, as flying use life energy and most people here have limited life energy. If during flight life energy is depleted down from a certain level then, the person will freeze in space there and medical staff will have to come there to refill the life energy of that person," she explained lucidly.

After that over some more height almost near clouds, those were very big clouds of white colour, spaceship-like vehicles were flying,

"So, the spaceship is also available here," I remarked.

"Of course, our kingdom is a quite developed one," she replied while rolling over her eye towards her forehead as generally, girls do.

After ascending above the cloud. A big floating island-like structure was visible, it was surrounded by a transparent boundary, which was shining on the surface, so although I was able to look inside, I could tell by seeing it that it was a boundary. On the island, there was a fort-like structure with many big and tall minarets. There was one big gate also for entering inside that fort.

"That is the headquarter of the defence department," said Hanna Tucker.

We went near the boundary. A small screen appeared on the boundary and a lady perhaps in her 50s appeared on that screen.

"Hello Miss Hanna, the first-class officer, what is the purpose of your visit in the headquarter of defence," asked that old lady. She was looking like some cruel granny of children stories. Few of her hairs were red and few white. She was a little oval-shaped and double-chinned.

"Hello, Mrs Edna Beckett, I am here to see our chief, Millicent Cooper. She had told me to pick up, this kind-hearted hero from the wishing well," said Hanna in a soft but confident manner.

"Very well," Edna Beckett said, "so what is the name of this kind-hearted hero," she asked.

"Ma'am," I said "My name is Ishaan Loknayak, and I am from another realm," I replied.

"Yes, young man," she replied, "my scan clearly shows that you are not from this realm, and you have an unusually high amount of life energy, that is very strange because this amount of life energy is possessed by very few individuals like our chief, the king of this kingdom and the other one is that black clocked evil person, we don't know his name although we only know this that, he wants to destroy our kingdom. That's why our chief was in the search of a hero, especially a kind-hearted hero who will save us from that evil creature."

"But ma'am," I said, "I don't know how to use my life energy how will I fight against that evil guy"?

"You will learn it soon," she said and pressed something as far as I could see on screen. A square opening emerged in the boundary. We entered the boundary and went toward the fort. We alighted near the main gate. From there we strolled inside. Two security guards were standing at the end of the main gate. The main gate was very high almost 50 feet in height and 20 feet in width. As we came near the main gate both guards saluted Miss Hanna Tucker and opened the gate. After entering the gate, a flying lift in the shape of a big box came toward us. It opened and we entered it. There was a talking panel inside the lift. A red laser light emerged from the panel and scanned the face of Hanna,

"Hello, Miss Hanna," a voice emerged from the panel. "Where do you want to go in the defence department?" it asked.

"Take us to the medicine department," said Hanna Tucker.

"Very well ma'am," reciprocated the panel of the lift. And it started flying. It flew right beneath designated wires for this purpose. The wire parted in many directions. Toward one of the directions, the lift turned swiftly. After a few seconds, it stopped near a gate. Over the gate it was written, Medicine department. We alighted there and entered inside the medicine department. As we entered the department of medicine a big, tall man with a long beard and small face appeared before us. He was slim and brawny. Although his face was small, his eyes were big.

"Hello Miss Hanna, how are you," said that tall man.

"Hello, Sir Ron Wilson," said Hanna than she looked toward me and continued saying, "he is the kind-hearted hero, I have brought him so that he can meet the chief as the chief has asked me to bring him to her."

"Very well," said Ron Wilson, "follow me."

While on the way going toward the room where Millicent cooper was resting, she looked at me and said,

"Mr Ron Wilson is the personal bodyguard of our chief. He is very strong. He is a level third citizen and class second officer, a class above me." She was smiling while saying so. Mr Ron Wilson also looked at me and he also tried to grin, due to which his long teeth were visible and one of the front teeth was black giving him a wicked look.

After a few seconds, we entered a room. It was a big room, as we entered from the gate a bed was laid on the left-hand side beside the wall, where the chief was resting. A nurse was also attending her, she was sitting beside the bed. Aiden Cox was also right behind us.

She stood up seeing Hanna and greeted her.

"Ma'am, the condition of the chief is stable now. She is sleeping right now if you say I should awake her," said the nurse.

"No Miss Jenifer," Hanna replied "I will myself awake her. And meet this gentleman from another realm," she pointed toward me and continued, "he is the kind-hearted hero, whom chief has asked me to fetch to her from the wishing well."

"Hello, kind-hearted sir," Jennifer looked at me and said while lowering her gaze. Then she turned to Hanna and said, "can I take leave now ma'am."

"Yes, you can," said Hanna. Jennifer left the room. Then Hanna looked toward me and said, "she is the head nurse of this medicine department."

"Ok," I replied. Then she went beside the chief. Chief was taking a rest while her eyes were closed.

"Hello ma'am, I have brought kind-hearted hero as you commanded me to do," said Hanna,

Listening to this the chief opened her eyes immediately and looked toward her then she looked toward me and replied,

"Very well done, Hanna, did any of the men of that wretched cloaked evil man follow you?" she seemed concerned about us.

"No ma'am," Hanna replied reassuring the chief, "we were not followed," the chief looked toward me and said.

"Kind-hearted hero, you should help us. There is a legend in this world that a kind-hearted hero from another realm only can help us. Especially the one whose heart is pure. A man whose heart is pure can only pass through the wishing well and come to our realm,"

"I can understand what you want to say ma'am, but I don't have any power how I can help you?" I replied.

"I'm sure that only you can help us,"

Then she looked toward Hanna and said further,

"Have you measured his level of citizenship through talking sphere of judgement?"

"No ma'am," replied Hanna, "I thought first I should get him to meet you."

"Then," the chief said, "do it now go to the measurement chamber and check his level."

"Yes ma'am," Hanna replied while saluting chief.

Hanna took me to the measurement chamber. Aiden Cox stayed outside as a maximum of two persons were allowed inside the measurement chamber. There was a big glass sphere in the middle of the chamber. We went close to the sphere. She looked at me and said,

"Put your right hand over this sphere and it will measure your life energy and the level of your citizenship."

"All right, here I go," I said and put my hand on the sphere. A screen appeared on the sphere and a voice emerged from it which was reading whatever was on screen.

"Scanning for the amount of life energy," the voice came out of the sphere. It was a male voice and a deep one. After a few seconds. "The amount of life energy seems exceptional almost equal to the life energy of the chief, but it seems it is locked inside the body that's why you are not able to use it."

Hanna looked at me with surprise.

"So, you might be the hero, after all, I had my doubts," then she looked to the sphere and said, "now measure how many fundamental forces of nature he can control."

"Yes, ma'am," said sphere, "measuring."

After a few minutes of measurement, a panicked voice emerged from the sphere.

"How can this be possible? It is impossible. How can a mere mortal possess such power?" blabbered the sphere.

"What happened, tell me?" Asked Hanna, she was disturbed listening to the panicked voice of the sphere.

"Yeah, tell me," I also said then the sphere replied,

"You can control all the fundamental forces of nature; in other words, you are even above fifth level citizen, and you are a god."

"What nonsense," I replied, "you must have measured me in the wrong way," while Hanna was staring toward me with utter disbelief and said,

"This sphere does not measure wrong ever. You could be a god, just you have not unlocked your potentials," said Hanna.

"No, that is not possible, I am not god. I am an ordinary man and I cannot even use any power of your realm; how can I be God? Tell me."

"I don't know about that, let's ask the chief what she will say about it."

CHAPTER 5: A GREAT APPREHENSION

Hanna and I left the measurement chamber and hurried to the chief. Aiden Cox also followed us who was standing outside the gate. While entering the room where the chief was resting, Hanna stopped momentarily and looked toward Aiden and said, "you should stay here, we have to talk about some important matter with the chief."

"Yes, ma'am," replied Aiden, "I shall wait here."

We both entered the room. Seeing me the chief smiled and said,

"So, both of you returned," and asked me, "did you get to know what your level of citizenship and energy level is?"

"Yes," I replied "but I think the measuring sphere has done a mistake. It has measured my life energy to be equal to almost yours, here I cannot even use life energy and about my citizenship level, it is saying that I am at the level of God, even higher than a fifth level citizen. I think it has made mistake in analyzing me."

Chief looked at Hanna and asked,

"What do you think about it?"

Hanna replied, "I don't know, as far as I know, the measuring sphere never does a wrong measurement. It has been accurate all the time, it might be the case that the kind-hearted hero is from another realm, so he is not able to use his life energy."

"That may be the case," said the chief, as both of them were only calling me a kind-hearted hero, I interrupted them and said,

"Please do call me with my name, it is Ishaan, you know it."

"Ok, Ishaan," said Hanna with a smile on her face. Then she turned to the chief and asked, "what should we do now?"

"let me think," said the chief, "even my level is fourth, and if measuring sphere says that Ishaan is at god level that means he has an even higher level than our king, Justin Edgar, he is at fifth level, only he can tell anything about Ishaan, as there is a rule in our kingdom that to decide anything about a citizen the level of the person who'd decide must be higher than the citizen about which he is deciding, as there is no level higher than god so, I think we must send Ishaan to the king, only he will decide about his fate here in this realm, and also I think Ishaan will require some training to use all of his controlling abilities as everyone take time to control fundamental forces. It is only the gravitational force which does not require any training."

"Yes ma'am" replied Hanna "but the training to use other forces besides the gravitational force is given in master's degree, to the selected one according to their level,"

"I have done graduation of my world, by the way, I have not done masters of there, is master of here is different in this realm?" I asked.

"Yes" replied Hanna, "it is different here, only citizens of level second and above are admitted in masters here. So, they can learn how to use powers corresponding to their level."

"All right then," said the chief, "first get him to meet with the king then get him admitted to master's degree course in the academy of fundamental powers."

"All right ma'am," said Hanna and saluted chief, I also saluted her.

We came out of head-quarter in the flying car of Hanna, her flying car was parked inside the Head-Quarter. She took me to her home. She said that I must have been tired of all the things that happened to me that day. She introduced me to her mother, whose name was Olivia Tucker, she was a little chubby lady but had a funny attitude. Her husband, James Tucker was also in the defence department, he was a second class officer. But he went on missing about 6 months ago. In her home, she lived with her mom and one servant only. After dinner, she gave me a room in her home for rest. While I was laying in my bed she came to my room. She sat beside me while I was laying in bed, being wrapped in a sheet made of pure silk-like substance. She looked at me with a smile and said,

"So, are you in a comfortable position now?"

"Yeah, quite comfortable. But I have lots of questions and worries also. I know nothing about your kingdom. And I am worried about my parents also."

"I can understand that," she replied, "let me tell you everything about my kingdom, in fact about my world."

"Go on, I am listening," I smiled while saying so and looked at her. She also chuckled a bit.

"Well," she said. "Our world is flat one not like your world, which is almost spherical one and another thing is that only anything living or dead can cross from your world to our world and go back also but anything from our world cannot cross to your world. There is one condition for crossing, that any citizen of level four or above, like our chief, did for saving you but that person will have to lose all her life energy. That's why our chief had to lose all her life energy when that black-cloaked guy tried to kill you in the dream."

"So that was a dream, but how can I die if someone kills me in a dream," I asked. Knowing that somebody could be killed in a dream was a piece of shocking news for me.

"Yeah, that was a dream but not an ordinary dream, it was a casted dream induced by secret force usage. Only a few people can use secret force and this secret force gives different power to different persons. That cloak guy uses this secret force as dream casting. So, he is a caster of the dream. He can enter any person's dream and kill that guy inside the dream. After that, that person's body will just disappear, as if it never existed in the real world," she said in a serious tone even I became serious listening to this.

"That's very dangerous power I think then," I spoke

"Yep, it is a very dangerous power, no one can tell what actual power a secret force user can possess. Till now only two people possessed this power. The first one is king, Justin Edgar and the second one is that the cloaked guy. Now you have become a user of this power, but you will require training. Yet if anyone came to know about this then this will greatly disturb the balance of powers in this world," she said.

"So, is there any connection between the king and that black-cloaked guy?" I asked.

"I don't know," she said and stopped for a moment.

"Well then," I gazed at her with an innocent look of mine and said, "tell me about your world and your kingdom in detail."

"In this world," she said with a deep breath, "we have nine kingdoms in total and a dark land on the westernmost part. Area wise that dark land is almost equal to all other nine kingdoms. It is separated by an invisible boundary of some kind of unknown forces, it is said that if anyone even looks at that boundary he will instantly disintegrate, it might be only a myth but no one dares to see the boundary. Only level five or above citizens can cross it, that's also a myth and the king only can cross it and that black-cloaked guy, of course, the king has never tried to cross the boundary but since he is a fifth level citizen he might cross. It is said that due to exposure to dark forces there, and the origin of dark forces is completely unknown, various types of evil creatures have appeared on dark land, and black-cloaked man, might be king of them. My kingdom is in the centre of this world in the eastern part. Other kingdoms surround it. The name of my kingdom is the Kingdom of Endora. Our kingdom is divided into 10 provinces each being administered by a governor appointed by his majesty king Justin Edgar. We are currently in province Lukemania, headquarter of defence department is also here. The capital of our kingdom is province Crownsing, it is a large town and known for tourism. The kings castle float in the sky there just like the department of defence here. And about people of our world, they are almost, look wise like people of your world, so that's a rough summary of our world. Do you want to ask anything else?

"No, thanks for all the info," I said while yawning, "I will ask later anything which I will not be able to understand."

"All right," she said with a chuckle, "good night."

"Good night," I replied, and she left the room.

***

The next day Hanna and I left for the capital just after having breakfast in the flying car of Hanna. It was a long journey through the sky, amongst the cloud. It took almost 3 hours to reach the capital, Crownsing. Hanna took the car to the castle. The castle was also floating on an island-like structure, but it was almost 10 times bigger than the floating island of the defence department. We entered the castle. Hanna arranged a meeting with the King, His highness Justin Edgar.

It was a big hall with a central table and chairs all around it. The design of the central table and chairs were mesmerizing, straight out of historic period drama movies. Fine handicrafts were done on them in golden colour depicting various flying creatures with wings, looking like dragons. The walls of the hall were also designed with extreme care and perfection. On all sides, big paintings were hung, I think they were the ancestors of the royal families.

After waiting for some time, the king came by the other gate, which I think only the king had the right to use. He was accompanied by almost, 20 guards and one head guard of that unit.

"Your highness," Hanna stood up seeing the king. I also stoop up and repeated the same words. The king was a muscular man of almost 7 feet in height. More than one foot taller than me. He was covered with body-protecting gears. On his head was a diamond-studded crown.

"The chief of defence department has sent me to you with the kindhearted hero, who can save the kingdom from the evil forces," as Hanna was saying this she was interrupted rudely by the king as he said,

"What rubbish, now this kind-hearted hero will save us, I am the highest level citizen in this kingdom with the fifth level and do you think that I need the help of this small fragile guy in saving my kingdom." the king was visibly in bad mood.

"But sir," said Hanna, "the sphere of measurement told that this man has a level above you and might be equal to the level of a god."

"What!" king become anxious and looked toward me and he said, "then prove to me that your level is above mine level."

"Your highness," I said, "I am not from this realm, I am from another realm, and I think that's why I am not able to use my life energy. Forget about showing my level to you, sir."

"Oh, I see," said the king and sat down on the biggest chair in the hall. And he looked to us, "take a seat, be at ease."

We sat down. Then he further said,

"So, what is your name, kindhearted hero?"

"Your highness, my name is Ishaan Loknayak," I said.

"That's a very strange name, it proves that you are not from this world," King chuckled. Then he looked at Hanna and asked,

"So why the chief has sent you along with Ishaan here?"

"Your highness," replied Hanna, "as the sphere of measurement put the level of citizenship of Ishaan above the fifth level so only you can decide what should be done to him, by the way, the chief also said that Ishaan must be admitted to the academy of fundamental powers."

"Very well," said the king, "then I bestow all the responsibility of Ishaan upon you."

"Yes, your highness," replied Hanna, "what are the commands for me about Ishaan then, sir."

"Firstly," said the king, "get Ishaan admitted to Academy of fundamental powers so that he could learn how to use fundamental forces, and I appoint you his assistant from now on as his level is above than that of yours and even above than that of me according to the sphere of measurement, I think you will not mind it, will you?"

"Of course not, your highness," said Hanna. Then the king asked Hanna to wait outside and told all his guards and including that head guard to wait outside as he had to talk some important things to me. When everyone left the hall. King stood up from his seat, so I also stood up. He came near me and said.

"Show me your hand Ishaan."

I held my hand in front of him. He held my hand with his right hand and started staring at me. His eyes became completely dark black and black mist appeared all around us. For a few seconds, he was in this condition and then, he let go off my hand and went again toward his seat and sat down while whispering to himself something.

"Pardon me, your highness, did you say something to me?" I asked in a humble tone.

"No nothing, that's none of your concern," said the king, "now please sit down Ishaan."

"Your highness," I said and sat down on the chair in front of the table.

"Well," said the king, "what chief has told you, tell me in detail don't hide anything."

"Sir," I said, "the chief said that your world is in grave danger and only a kindhearted hero like me can save your world from grave danger, I think that black-cloaked guy might be the sole cause of all the danger to your world."

"And do you know who is that black-cloaked guy?" asked the king.

"No sir, I don't know, no one knows about him I think," I replied.

"I knew the chief will not tell you and I am sure that chief has nefarious planning against me, I just don't have enough evidence against her otherwise I would kill her," said the king in an extremely angry voice.

"Sir," I said, "I did not understand what you are saying? Are you saying that the chief of the defence department is conspiring against you? That is a very big and serious accusation against her."

"Ishaan," said the king, "that is very unfortunate, but it is true, my spies have told me so, and the cloaked guy is also relative of the chief."

"What," I became shocked after listening to this, "if this is the case then why she did not tell me?"

"That is very much clear," said the king, "because she is conspiring against me, she wants to overthrow me and put that cloaked guy on the throne, one of my spies has seen once the chief and the cloaked guy talking to each other and then they hugged each other, why any lady would hug any stranger, only if that stranger is some relative of her. And I also feel that the cloaked guy is her father because the cloaked guy came to be seen one year after the disappearance of her father Henry Cooper, who was my prime minister and fourth level fundamental force user citizen, although I doubted that he was the fifth level."

"Well," I asked, "what should I do then?"

"First of all, play along with the chief and do as she says you to do," said the king, "and work as a spy for me, and if you see any unusual activity then press the button of this device it will record whatever would be happening all around you and record as evidence so that I can persecute the chief for her crime against the kingdom of Endora. As I uphold the law and order under all circumstances, so I need strong evidence against her. I just cannot act against her on my whim." The king gave me a cubical shaped device with a red button on it on one side and he said further,

"And you will not tell anyone what I have told you here. The chief might get you killed if she comes to know that you have become my spy, and be aware of that lady Hanna, I think she also works for the chief, that's why I have made her your assistance by a royal decree. Now she will have to follow you only. You can try to convince her so that she does not follow that wicked chief, am I clear to you?"

"Yes, your highness," I said, "I understood everything, I will report directly to you and none."

"Very well Ishaan," said the king and he gave me a shining batch, it was made of the purest and highest quality of diamond, and he said further, "this is royal entry pass, if you show this pass to anyone, he will not stop you from going to any sensitive area, even coming to me directly."

"Thank you, your highness," I said, "that's very great honour you have bestowed on me," while taking the diamond batch. Then the king asked me to take my leave.

I came out of the hall and met Hanna. She was waiting for me outside the hall patiently. While looking at me she blushed,

"So, what did his highness, told to you," She asked while we were slowly walking toward her flying car.

"Nothing special," I said, "just man to man fun talk."

"Oho, fun talk with king, really," she said while giggling.

"Yes," I said, "after all my level is higher than him," listening to this she had a great laugh such that people walking around us started looking at her. She stopped laughing feeling a little awkward at herself. We both entered the flying car and flew out of the king's castle.

"So, I am your assistance now, what is your order for me," she smiled while saying so.

"Oh please," I said, "you are like my friend, how can I order you."

"But the king has appointed me your assistance, now I will have to call you sir," she said

"Don't bother with that," I replied, "just call me Ishaan, and as you have lots of experience of this world, it would be better if you guide me, Hanna."

She looked at me and blushed, "ok, Ishaan. first of all, let me get you admitted to the academy of fundamental powers. there, you will learn controlling fundamental powers then only you will be helpful to the department of defence in fighting the black-cloaked guy."

"Very well," I said, "then let's go to the academy of fundamental powers.

"Yes sir," she replied and blushed. I looked at her with an angry look. After that look of mine. She laughed again and said, "wow! You look so cute in this angry young man look. Just incredible."

"Really?" I asked

"Yes, absolutely," she said with her evergreen smile. I also smiled at her. Now we were going toward the academy of fundamental powers. Although I was smiling at her but deep inside, I was in great fear. The way the king told me that the chief and the black-cloaked guy are related to each other was filling my heart with apprehension and some darkness within. I was doubting Hanna also. I was in a great dilemma then. I started to doubt the motives of everyone there. And if the king was saying truth why would the chief invite me to save the Kingdome from that cloaked guy if that cloaked guy is a relative of the chief. My heart was aching. My heart was saying that I should tell Hanna what the king had told me, but my mind was warning against it, my mind was saying if the king had told the truth, then telling Hanna would result in the immediate demise of me as till then I had not grasped any knowledge of using fundamental forces of nature. If I would tell Hanna all the things and if those things whatever, the king had told me were true then Hanna might try to kill me. I was having all types of dreadful thoughts. Initially, I thought that this world was so wonderful, so scientific and so advanced and now I came to realize that there is much darkness beneath all those glittering external appearances. Although I was in great apprehension, only time would tell me what actuality was or what was fallacious.

CHAPTER 6: MY FIRST FLIGHT

We entered the academy of fundamental powers in the flying car of Hanna. We entered the office of the principal of the academy.

"May I come in," said Hanna to the principal.

The principal was signing some documents on his desk. He was an old guy with overgrown white hair and a small skull cap on his head having some handicraft all over it. While he was signing documents with his right hand there was a cigar in his left hand. His outfit was loose, and he looked like some grandpa. He had a small beard and no moustache. He looked at Hanna over his specs as specs were at a lower portion of his nose.

"Hello, miss Hanna, come in, come in please have seat," said the principal. I along with Hanna went inside the principal's office and sat down on the visitors' chair. On the name plate on the desk of the principal, his name was written, it was **Mr** Charles Acosta, Principal, Level third citizen.

"Well, Miss Hanna, would you like to have some drink hot or cold?" asked Mr Charles.

"No, thanks," replied Hanna and pointing toward me she said, "he is the kind-hearted hero."

"Hello, young man, the chief has already told me about you over telepathy, level three and above can use telepathy, by combining electric and magnetic force, hence they can send message directly into the mind of receiver of any level."

"I am much-obliged sir," I replied.

"So, I admit you in the first year of three-year master's course of controlling fundamental forces"

"Thank you, sir," I said "I will do my best in course, sir."

Mr Charles looked at Hanna and said, "Miss Hanna you can complete the admission formalities of our kind-hearted hero, I mean Ishaan Loknayak," then he looked toward me and smiled, "of course chief told me your name," I also smiled in anticipation.

After that Miss Hanna helped me complete my admission formalities. I was also provided with a hostel there. The hostel was decided according to the level of students and according to the talking sphere my level was even above fifth, so I was to choose my hostel block at my discretion. I thought it would be a good idea not to show off, so I preferred level third hostel block.

In this block, all students had level three citizenship that means they can control electric force and magnetic force along with gravitational force.

I entered the block of level third students. The main gate was elegantly designed with woodcraft having caricatures of different mythical beasts, I observed. Just after entering the main gate, the reception desk was there. Miss Hanna was also with me. We went near the reception desk. A young lady, in her thirties I assumed, was sitting there with a light touch of makeup on her face and overly applied blush on both cheeks. She looked at us and with a warm smile she said,

"Hello sir, and ma'am, how can I help you?"

"I got admission in the academy of fundamental powers, in the first year of three-year master's course of controlling fundamental force," I said while showing my id issued by the academy of fundamental forces.

"Very well," she said, "I am issuing a room for you." Within a few minutes, she issued a room for me and gave me a card to access the room. She looked at Hanna and asked,

"How, may I help you, ma'am?"

"I am assistant to Mr Ishaan, duly appointed by his Excellency, our king and I am a first-class officer in the department of defence," replied Hanna.

"All right then," she replied, "have a nice day both of you," then she rang a bell placed at her desk. An old lady, perhaps in her fifties having old fashioned frock guise came there.

"Yes, Daisy ma'am," she said, "what is your order for me, ma'am"

"Meet Mr Ishaan Loknayak and his assistant Miss Hanna Tucker," Daisy said, "Mr Ishaan is the first-year student of the master's course of controlling fundamental forces, I have allotted room for him, please help him in finding his allotted room."

"Yes, ma'am," she replied. While looking at me, she said, "Sir, kindly follow, me. My name is Talia Hodge and I work as Helper Lady in this Hostel."

"It's my pleasure to meet you, ma'am," I replied while I started following her. Hanna also started to follow me but was stopped by Daisy, "Ma'am, only students are allowed beyond this point,"

Hanna smiled at her and said, "it's ok ma'am" then she looked at me and gave me a mobile-like device. Just then I remembered that I had lost my mobile somewhere, I did not remember clearly where though.

"Just say my name in this device to contact me, all right. I know you will soon learn telepathy although," she chuckled.

I took the device, "yeah, sure. Thanks."

"Bye, all the best for your masters," she replied with her usual appealing beam.

Mrs Talia took me to the room on the fifth floor. It was a medium-sized room with the facility of staying two students. Two beds were there on side of the walls.

There were two study tables for each roommate. There was an attached bathroom.

When I entered the room, my roommate was studying a book while lounging on his bed. He glanced at me briefly and then he submerged into his book again. I thought him to be some nerdy student. Look wise he was a little fair and with a slightly reddish flair in his hair. His nose was a little broad, and his chin was sharp. He was wearing specs.

"Sir, make yourself comfortable. If you need anything you can inform the reception," said Mrs Talia and she left. I sat on the other bed and looked at my strange, reticent roommate.

"Hello," I said while looking at him, "My name is Ishaan, and I am not from this realm, I have come from another realm."

He glanced at me and smirked, "don't crack a joke, there is no realm other than this realm, only in stories other realms exists," and he turned toward his book again, "by the way my name is Nathan Adams, and please don't disturb me with your stupid talks, and your stupid name as well."

I somehow felt a little humiliated at his behaviour but then I also stretched down over my bed.

***

It was a large assembly hall of the academy. The principal had gathered along with all faculty teachers at the stage and students were sitting at chairs which were laid around big square tables. There were almost 15 tables arranged in rows of five tables. On the first row table, newly admitted students were sitting. I was also sitting along with them. In the second row, the second-year students were sitting and in the third row, the third-year students were sitting.

The principal started his speech.

"I welcome all twenty new students in this prestigious academy for controlling fundamental powers. As everyone knows that only citizens of level second or higher are accepted in this master's degree course of ours academy so there are very few numbers of students in our academy. This year only twenty students got admitted in the first year. Out of which fifteen are level second students, four are level third students and one is level five student," as soon as the principal announced this, there ensued an uproar throughout the hall. "Silence," the principal raised his voice, "now I will introduce all faculty members including myself to all new students of the master degree course," the principal cleared his throat and said once again, "My name is Charles Acosta and I am third level citizen, I will teach all of you fundamental of life energy and how to control life energy for using fundamental forces of nature, now one by one other faculty members will introduce themselves to all of you."

Firstly, a lady stood up she was sitting on the leftmost chair on the stage and the principal was sitting in the middle chair. She was a middle-aged lady elegantly dressed in one of the finest fabrics of that realm. She was wearing a round hat with artificial flowers on it. She chuckled a bit while standing up and started saying, "Hello, new students of this prestigious academy. I must say that it is the luck of all of you to get a chance of joining here. My name is Tilly Kelly. I am a second class citizen. I will teach all of you how to control the electric force of nature, get ready for lightning and thunder," while saying so she chuckled once again and along with her students also laughed. Although she was talking on stage and looking at almost every student, she had a particular gaze of her toward me. While sitting down on her chair she almost started staring at me for a few seconds then after that, she drifted her gaze away from me. Maybe she knew my level of citizenship but she never disturbed me after that creepy stare or maybe that was unintentional, I just don't know.

In the same way faculty members introduced themselves. After the introduction of faculty members there came the turn of new students to introduce themselves. First, my roommate stood up and started to introduce himself.

"Hello, everyone, my name is Nathan Adams, and I am a level-three citizen," after saying so he sat down. Everyone started whispering after listening to his name. I doubted there must be a story about it, and I must ask him. After him, 18 more students introduced themselves. Then came my turn. I started introducing myself, "My name is Ishaan Loknayak, and I don't know my level currently," although I was the last student, so everyone was expecting me to say the fifth level, but I intentionally tried to hide my level. The fact was that I was not even able to use my life energy would come as a humiliation to me soon, I thought. I continued speaking, "since I have got admission to this academy, I can say that my level is at least two."

***

It was the first class of the day and the principal himself entered the class as it was a class of controlling the life energy and maximizing it. As soon as the principal entered the class everyone stood up.

"Sit down," said the principal. I was seated in the front row. A beautiful girl was seated right beside me. Her name was Isabel Hurst. She introduced herself to me while we entered our first class.

"So how are all of you feeling? Eager to improve your control over life energy and to increase it in your body. I hope all of you must know how to use this for controlling fundamental forces of nature according to your level," as he was saying this, I raised my hand, "Yes Mr Ishaan, level five citizen, what do you want to say?"

"Sir," I replied, "although the measuring sphere has pronounced my level to be five, I have doubt." Every student in the class was staring at me. Isabel was also staring at me.

"Yes, ask what your doubt is," enquired the principal.

"Sir," I responded. "I don't know how to use my life energy." As soon as I pronounced this everyone busted into laughter except Isabel. She became curious and started gazing at me as if she had lots of questions for me in her mind.

"It is very simple Mr Ishaan, don't be afraid of it," consoled the principal, "stand up and come to me, I will right now teach you how to use your life energy and how to know how much life energy you possess."

I stood up from my seat and went near the principal. "Now Ishaan, face toward your classmates." Said, the principal. I stood there facing classmates. "Now close your eyes and try to locate your life energy in the darkness you see while closing your eyes," said the principal.

"Yes sir," while saying so I closed my eyes. After a few minutes of trying hard. still, I was not able to see anything. "Sir, I can't see anything. Please tell me more specifically how to see life energy," I asked.

"It seems your life energy is blocked. I will have to unblock it by forcing some of my life energy into you. The main point of entering and controlling life energy lies in the centre of the forehead, now try to focus there while closing your eyes while I impart some of my life energy into you," said the principal.

I focused hard on the centre of my forehead. I was feeling some light entering my body, perhaps as the principal was imparting some of his life energy to me. After focusing for a few minutes, a large sphere of light appeared in front of me in the darkness.

"Sir I can see a sphere of light. Very bright light. Is it life energy?" I asked while still my eyes being closed.

"Yes" replied the principal. "Now slowly open your eyes and try to see that energy outside and try to control basic forces of nature using that energy."

I opened my eyes and tried to emulate the sphere in front of me, within a few seconds a large sphere of light appeared in front of me, it was huge. It was extending way beyond the classroom. Bypassing the walls of the class. Seeing this all other students became nervous and frightened. The principal also became astonished seeing this. After a few seconds, I lost concentration and the sphere disappeared.

"You have a very high level of life energy almost equal to the king of our kingdom," said the principal. "Now in other classes, you will learn how to control fundamental forces using your life energy," the time of his class ended, and he left. I sat down in my seat.

"Wow! That was awesome," said Isabel, "I have to ask lots of questions to you, will you talk with me after classes," she asked while blushing.

"Sure," I said.

After two more classes recess ensued. I along with Isabel went toward the canteen of the academy. She brought a dish almost like a sandwich of my world that is earth, for herself and me. We took a seat there and started eating that sandwich like dish.

"Hmm," while eating she said "well Ishaan, your name is strange. Are you from some other country?"

"The fact is a little stranger than that, if I tell you, you will not believe me," I said.

"Go on. Try telling your origin story, only then I will say that It is strange or not," she said while chuckling.

"Well," I cleared my throat and continued, "I am not from this world, I am from another realm. In my realm there exist no such energy as life energy. And In fact, I don't know anything about this life energy. In my realm, no one can control fundamental forces of nature."

She was looking at me in amazement. "I knew it," she said, "the first time I saw you, I knew that you are not from this world," she smiled.

"And about life energy, we study about that in graduation course," she said further, "as you are from another world that's why you don't know about it, I think."

"So," I said, "can you tell me about it?"

"Yes sure," she said while finishing her sandwich, I also had finished my sandwich by then.

"Our body possesses two types of energy," she explained, "both of these energies are stored in mitochondria. Normal mechanical energy is stored in ATPs and life energy is stored in APPs. You must have a large number of APPs in your mitochondria. That's why you possess so much of life energy," she was blushing while explaining.

"Thank you for explaining life energy," I said, "can you also explain how to use life energy to control gravitational force. Because everyone knows this here and I don't know this."

She chuckled a bit and replied, "it is very simple, just visualize life energy in whatever form such that you can pull or push the mass of any object around you then use that imaginative object or process to control the gravitation."

"I did not understand, can you show how you control gravitation force using your life energy," I asked.

"Well let's go to the field, there I will demonstrate everything."

We both stood up and started going toward the field of the academy. On the way, a rude student collided with Isabel.

"I am sorry," she said but the other guy was visibly fuming he uttered some slang words I think, and spoke.

"What rubbish, how such low-grade citizens like you get admitted in this academy, such pathetic people," he said while looking toward Isabel. I remembered his name was Kira Calhoun and he was a third level citizen. He behaved haughtily in the introduction as well.

"Wait a minute," I interrupted "why are you saying so to her, you must apologize to her now."

"Oho," he said while looking at me, "I don't even talk to a lowly creature like her," I became furious listening to this I was about to say something but Isabel held my hand and said, "leave him alone, he is a loser," and while almost pulling away from him she further said,

"Let's go to the field."

We went to the field. It was a very big field with lush green grass on it which was evenly cut. She gazed at me and said, "well Ishan I assume my life energy is as hooks attached with my body which interact with the space-time continuum and hence, I fly, see"

Few bright hooks appeared around her body those hooks were sticking in space as if it is a solid substance, hooks were attached to the body of Isabel. She slowly lifted upward. Then she said, "we can also make these constructs invisible," and all those hooks disappeared. She came back to the ground. By seeing this demonstration, I understood one thing. Life energy can be moulded into various shapes and hence it can be used in doing various things. I thought of using my experience of my world and tried to make things of my world in that realm. And for flying what is better than a rocket engine. "I should also try then; I have an idea," I said to Isabel.

"Yes, you should try to make anything with your life energy that can help you in flying."

"Yeah, sure," I looked at her and smiled, "wish me luck."

"Best of luck," she chuckled.

I collected life energy in front of me and converted it into a rocket engine. I thought it to be the two-sided engine, for acceleration and deceleration. I used my concentration power to fit this life energy made rocket engine behind my back. I thought life energy to collect some oxygen and hydrogen from the atmosphere, at this stage I was unknowingly using my fourth level power which I later came to know. My life energy rocket engine was ready now. I made it invisible by bending lights around it. Which was also a use of second and third level force unknowingly although I later came to know that life energy can be made hidden from others sight without the use of other forces.

I started my rocket engine and zoom, within a few seconds I was in the sky. Amongst the cloud. Isabel was also chasing me, but she took her time. I became stationary near the cloud so that Isabel could come to me.

"Wow! Slow down Ishaan, I cannot fly so fast," she said while chuckling. I slowed down the burning speed of hydrogen. Then we both flew for some time. I was enjoying my first flight immensely.

CHAPTER 7: APATOR: A SOUL-LESS CREATURE

Within a few months, I was able to use electric force and magnetic force. Using a combination of these forces now I was able to talk telepathically with Hanna and Isabel and in fact with anyone whom I had met once. I was also able to search for anyone using facial recognition within an area of 2 km around me.

One evening when I was having fun while flying over cloud alone, I saw Nathan going somewhere in a strange way. The way he was walking seemed as if he was frightened by something. I hid under optical illusion by combining electro and magnetic forces. I started following him. He also started flying but at a low height. I came just a few meters behind him. He entered a big black old house. In the house, some clamour I was hearing in feeble amplitude. I amplified it using electric force and now I was able to hear it. It was the black clocked guy that was talking to him. Black cloaked guy seemed quite angry with Nathan, he shouted in anger and said,

"What do want after all? Don't you want that, I must leave the body of your brother? I am having a feeling, I think you don't love your brother?"

"No, this is not true, I love my brother and I can do anything to save him," Nathan was sobbing profusely, a low thud I was able to hear, I thought, Nathan has fallen on his knees.

"Then how much more time will you take in doing such petty work of me. Until you don't do this I will not leave the body of your brother," after saying so, the blacked cloaked guy laughed in the cruellest way possible.

Then a sound of gusting wind I heard as if the black-cloaked guy disappeared in the air.

****

The next day I went to see Hanna in her home. It was the time of evening. She was making tea for her mother and herself. I knocked on the gate. She opened the gate. She was wearing a fine dress of pink colour.

"I hope I have not disturbed you coming at this time," I said while smiling.

"Of course not. Please come in," she replied.

She took me to the guest room. "Take your seat, I will bring tea for you," she said.

"No please don't get yourself troubled," I replied.

"There is no trouble in this, I have already made tea," she responded and sprinted toward the kitchen. After a few minutes, she put a cup of tea in front of me and sat beside me.

"So, how is your study going, what things have you learned, tell me?" She asked in a humble and pleasing voice.

"Well," I said, "I have learned how to control electric and magnetic forces that you already know as I have talked with you through telepathy, have you forgotten?" I asked while showing a little pretentious anger.

"No," she raised her voice a little bit then again she calmed her voice, "I meant to ask what other things have you learnt, by the way, generally students take the whole first year in controlling electric force, and here you have learnt to control both electric and magnetic force in the first year only. That's a very big achievement and it also proves that you are at least a third level citizen so I can now surely be your assistant," she laughed after saying so.

"I have learned how to hide from view using electromagnetic force, in my realm, it is called an electromagnetic wave also, I can do a facial search, I can listen to the distant voice and I am also exploring what other things I can do," I said.

"Wow! That seems extraordinary," she screamed with astonishment.

"The thing is I have to ask you something if you don't mind. Can I?" I asked while looking at her. She blushed a bit and I became perplexed why she was blushing as I was going to ask only about Nathan and things that transpired between him and the black-cloaked guy. She lowered her gaze and said in a faint voice, "yes Ishaan, you can ask me, and you can propose me," while saying so she closed her eyes and covered her visage with palms.

"What!" was the words that came out of my mouth. Her mother also came running to the living room where we were sitting and shouted,

"What! You are going to propose my daughter?" she was gasping.

"Mom. Please go inside your room you are disturbing him. Leave him alone so that he could propose to me," said Hanna.

"No that is not what I have to ask," I stuttered a bit while saying so.

"See mom. He has got frightened because of you, please mom, go inside your room," Hanna raised her voice a bit but still in a polite way. Her mother left the room. She once again looked at me. "Don't be shy say it."

"You are misunderstanding me, Hanna," I replied, "I am not going to propose to you," I was going to say further but she interrupted me and spoke.

"Oh, I can understand it, don't say further anything. You have level three and might have level four or five and I am at only level two that's why you don't want to propose to me, never mind, I won't be upset because of it, I can understand. After all your level is much higher than that of mine how can you possibly propose a girl of lower level? I think you will only propose girls of a level equal to that of yours," while saying so she seemed a little upset.

"Oh god," I thought, *"by the way she is quite beautiful there is no harm in proposing her, and now I understood she liked me from the beginning that's why she always talked to me with so much enthusiasm, what a duffer I am, I was not able to understand this and also as almost every girl talk in a similar way to their friend-zoned friends so I did not suspect it."* Then I said, "I will propose you some other time surely, you are splendidly beautiful, but right now I have to ask you something else, this is something about my roommate in the hostel, his name is Nathan Adam." After listening to this she blushed

and then said, "all right, take your time but don't be much late okay."

"Okay, but can I tell you about Nathan?" I said in a little frustration.

"Yes," she granted her permission to me, "you can tell." She chuckled.

"Hmm," I cleared my throat I continued saying, "Nathan is my roommate, and he is a third level citizen. His behaviour is quite strange, and it seems he always remains angry over everyone around him. He doesn't even talk with anyone and talks very rarely only when it becomes utmost imperative. The other day he was going somewhere. It felt quite strange to me, so I followed him. He entered a black building. The building was quite old. In that building, the black-cloaked guy was also there." After listening to the black-cloaked term, her eyes grew larger. She fixated her all attention on me and asked, "Then what happened?"

"I listened to some of their conversations and came to know that black clocked guy is the brother of

Nathan I mean his brother's body is possessed by the soul of black-cloaked creature or whatever he is,"

"Oh my god," she replied in a great shock, "so it means the black-cloaked guy is using the body of brother of Nathan."

"Yes," I replied, "and that guy wanted something to be done by Nathan only then he will release the body of his brother. I want to ask you if you know anything about Nathan."

"I kind of have listened to this name somewhere but I don't remember exactly. We will have to look in the storage of Head Quarter. In the storage section of headquarter, every information about each individual of this kingdom is written in their family book."

"Family book?" I repeated with a sort of astonishment. I have many times listened to this term but always thought it to be some book for small children.

"Yes, now let's go," she chuckled and stood up.

We took the flying car and started flying toward the head quarter. Hanna parked her car in the parking, and we entered the hanging lift and told the lift our destination as storage. In a few seconds, we were near the gate of storage. Inside storage, big books were placed on big and tall racks. There were virtually innumerable racks of extreme height. The storage area was poorly lit, and it looked like a black and white big hall filled with book racks.

"What was the full name of Nathan, say again," she asked while looking at all those dreadful big racks.

"Mr Nathan Adams," I replied.

"So," she said, "we will have to look for rack where family books with letter A could be found, that is the family book of Adams,"

I looked clearly that each rack was named with a letter such as A, or B etc. I found a rack on which A was printed.

"Look there Hanna, A is printed on this rack" I shouted as Anna was at a distance from me and was searching on other racks. She came near me and looked at that. The height of the rack was extreme. The lower row was printed with 'Aa', upper 'Ab' and so on. Seeing this I inferred that we would have to fly upward to see the row having Ad on it. I looked at Hanna.

"I think we will have to fly upward to see row containing the name Adams."

"Yes," she replied. We both flew upward and reached the row containing books starting with the letters 'Ad'. After searching for a few seconds, I found the book on which 'Adams Family Book' was written. I looked at the book and showed it to Hanna. She nodded her head and said, "yep, that is the book we were searching for," we both alighted on the ground.

"Now we will know about Nathan completely," she said. I was about to open the book but just then a black mist appeared in front of me and then it took the visage of a man with black cuts all over his face. As it was a little dark there, so I was not able to perceive his identity. Then he came near me I almost froze. He took the book from me and transformed himself into black mist and went away along with the book.

"Ishaan, are you all right, that guy just snatched the book from you, now how will we be able to know about Nathan?" Hanna shouted. I was frozen after seeing his face for a few seconds. Then once again Hanna shouted,

"Are you alright Ishaan, what happened to you, do you know that Apator?"

I came to my senses and repeated the words of Hanna "Apator!" then I remembered that the Principal had already taught us about Apator. An Apator is a soulless body that can convert into a black dark force and can easily cross the boundary of the dark world and come into the world of nine kingdoms. Apators are created by chance only as no human being can cross towards the dark world. And no one knows how Apator is created in the dark world. It was a complete mystery.

"How can this be possible," I stuttered while saying so. "How can this be possible," I repeated. I became upset, and tears streamed out from my eyes over my cheeks.

"What happened, will you tell me?" screamed Hanna to me. I somehow held myself and then looked at Hanna. She hugged me trying to calm me.

"He was my friend in my world, my best friend, how this can happen to him," I almost choked while saying so.

"Oh, that is terrible, but how he entered the dark world. Apator can only be created when someone enters into the dark world, how your friend could have entered the dark world?"

"I don't know," I replied while still few drops of tears trickled over my cheeks, "he had jumped into the well before me, but he was not present there when I came out of the wishing well, I don't know how he entered the dark world."

"That is a very serious issue," Hanna said, "we must ask the chief about this, whether she knows it or not," we both headed toward the office of the chief.

She was still recovering but had recovered enough to start working in her office. As I opened the gate, she looked toward us and smiled, "come in Ishaan, come in." I along with Hanna entered the office of chief.

"Have seats," the chief said while still smiling.

"So how are you Ishaan?" and after gazing at Hanna, "how are you, Miss Hanna? I am aware that his Excellency has duly appointed you as personal assistant to Ishaan."

"I am fine ma'am," I replied and Hanna also replied, "I am fine ma'am and it's my honour to serve as personal assistant to Ishan after all he is above level five citizen, he has already mastered level three forces and I am sure soon he will master level five forces as well, I am proud of being his assistant."

Chief looked at me and with a humble tone, she remarked, "you look a little upset, what happened? Tell me."

"Ma'am," I replied "Hanna and I was looking for the family book of Adams when I found it. it was snatched from me by an Apator,"

"Oh," exclaimed the chief, "that is horrible, how can an Apator breach our headquarter? I will have to surely beef up securities here."

"yeah, ma'am that's quite concerning but more concerning is that the Apator had a similar face as that of my friend in my world who also fell into the wishing well before me, and I am extremely upset how he turned into an Apator, how he could have entered into the dark world, I am just not able to understand how this happened?"

"oh holy gods," uttered chief, "that is an extremely concerning issue, I think we will have to find out about the wishing well, there is a book about wishing well in our library, let's see if we get our answers in that. I am asking Ron, telepathically to bring it to me."

"Oh, I see" she exclaimed after a few minutes and said, "Ron is saying that the book of wishing well has been issued to the king, so we will have to visit kings castle to know about your friend, Ishaan."

"I will go myself," I said with a firm resolute, "you should take a rest, you have not fully recovered ma'am."

"All right but be careful, that cloaked guy might attack you," the chief said.

"Roger that ma'am" I replied.

Hanna and I took the flying car of Hanna and started our journey towards the capital. Within a few seconds, we were flying over white clouds. Various spaceships were visible in the background, and there, the first time I saw a cargo ship. It was a huge spaceship having the same shape as that of a submarine of my world but instead of being submersed into water, it was sailing above the clouds.

A lightning bolt appeared behind us. It was about to collide with our car. I created an electromagnetic defence boundary all around the car using all the practice that I did in the electromagnetic lab of the academy of higher education. Almost 15 black cars appeared behind us. They were following us and in all of them, black-cloaked peoples were present. They were continuously attacking us with lighting bolts. But they were not able to destroy the defence boundary created by me.

"Hanna, drive faster, we must lose them," I shouted

"I am trying," replied Hanna.

She flew the car in various directions. I also hit some of the black cars with electric bolts of my own. Few of them blasted in the air and others were still trailing us.

Then I used my life energy to mimic a large machine gun expelling energy bullets attached to the rear of the car. Using that Machin gun, I started firing energy bullets on all those black cars. They started blasting in the air. After a few seconds, only one car was in the air behind us, and it was withstanding my energy bullets.

"The last car is not going off our trail, I feel it is the real one, real black-cloaked guy," I said to Hanna while pumping a few more energy bullets toward the last black car but that black guy deflected it using some kind of barrier.

"Yeah, he seems real black-cloaked guy that attacked our chief in your dream in your world, it would be very difficult for us to get rid of him."

Black cloaked guy collected electromagnetic energy over his palm and attacked us. I also collected some electromagnetic energy and countered that attack. Both energies collided mid-air. Our car was ahead going to the capital. Black cloaked guy's car was following us, and the electromagnetic energy released by both of us were colliding mid-air. The black guy poured, perhaps, more of his life energy into creating stronger electromagnetic energy and his electromagnetic energy now was pushing my electromagnetic energy and the collision point was coming near our car. I got a little frightened seeing this.

"Hanna, could you help a little bit, that guy is overpowering me,"

"Wait," replied Hanna and she pulled the car aside line of attack and flew above the line of attack gaining some height while whirling rapidly. The black-cloaked guy did something and translucent arrows appeared all around his car and he struck us with those arrows. I created a defensive wall for containing those arrows but a few of them penetrated through my defence and hit the car. The car became unstable and started falling downward. Hanna and I abandoned the car and now we were flying above the clouds. Black cloaked guy's car came near us. I enacted a defence sphere all around me and Hanna. That cloaked guy started hitting us with arrows, electric sparkles and various other things. My defence circle was becoming weakened. It was about to shatter, just then a mysterious dot appeared in front of me, it was like a small sphere. I saw closely into it. I saw planet earth in this tiny sphere. As my defence sphere crackled due to the attack by that cloaked guy, the little sphere in front of me, swallowed me and Hanna into it, now we were falling, I was not able to use my life energy to control the gravitational field, and hence I was not able to fly. So was Hanna, not able to use her life energy. We both fell into a river. Although we did not fall from much height, we became unconscious.

CHAPTER 8: I AM BLACK CLOAKED DEVIL

When I came around, I was laying on the bed in a hospital. A nurse was checking equipment beside my bed. On the other bed in the same room, Hanna was laying. She was still unconscious. The nurse saw me and smiled, "so finally you became conscious. It took 3 hours. You and that lady along with you were drowning in the river, Yamuna. One of the fishermen saw you and her and pulled both of you in their boat. Both of you should be thankful to them they saved your life after all." After saying so she left the room. Hanna also woke up and got seated there. She saw me and the room in a strange and perplexing way.

"Where are we? Ishaan," she asked in great astonishment, "do you know this place; it has strange machinery here."

"Yeah, I know this place," I replied to Hanna, "this is the hospital of my world."

"What!" she exclaimed, "how can this be possible? We can't enter in your world using wishing well and also how can I enter your world, its against rule, you know,"

"Yeah," I replied while looking at her. She was sitting on the hospital bed and disconcertingly looking all around. "We have not come here using wishing well as far as I remember."

"Then how come we came here, can you explain this bizarre incident, a few moments ago we were being attacked by the black-cloaked devil and now we have entered your world. It's extremely strange to be true. Are we hallucinating ?" she gazed at me and asked exasperatingly.

"No, I don't think we are dreaming. As far as I can remember I saw a small sphere about the size of a water drop in front of me and that drop engulfed us, the next moment we fell in the river, that's all I remember," I replied to her.

"That seems like some portal, but who created that portal, did you create it by mistake unknowingly, after all, you are above level five citizen of my realm, perhaps you can do it and you just don't know it yet, to save me and yourself you might have accidentally created that portal to your world, what do you think about it?" she asked me excitingly.

"I don't know, but if we have come to my world then I don't think that we will be able to control fundamental forces of nature, in my world, neither life energy exists nor the fundamental forces of nature can be controlled by a human being, in other words, you and I both are powerless in this world," I explained to her our dire situation in the earthly realm.

"Yeah, I can feel so," Hanna replied with some nervousness, "I am not able to access my life energy here, forget about controlling fundamental forces of nature, I think APP are active only in my realm not in your realm."

"I also think so, but we will have to find a way to tackle that black-cloaked guy problem of your realm, I don't know how we will do it, in this earthly realm we are merely human beings devoid of any powers," I replied with an anxious facade.

"We will have to think about it, maybe we will find some way or we will have to use that wishing well to enter into our realm, I don't know whether that will work or not?" she asked.

"Maybe that will work. But now I have returned to my earth, so I don't think that I am in the mood of going in your realm again, although your realm is quite magical but, there is this black guy also there, I mean it's very risky," I said. "And also, my parents must be very anxious about me as I have not met them for almost one year now"

"I can understand your feeling but only you can save our world, there is a prophecy about you, only a kind-hearted hero can save my world, and also you are a level five citizen, please don't abandon us," she said with a gloomy face and came near me, she held my hands and further said, "please help us."

"All right," I replied, she blushed a bit, "first, let's get out of this hospital, then we will visit my home after that we will think about how to get back into your world and fight that black-cloaked guy." She beamed once again and replied "okay,"

After completing a few formalities, we got discharged from the hospital. I along with her started proceeding toward my home. I gave the universal translator to Hanna because here she needed that.

***

I rang the bell of my house. After some time, Roshni, my sister opened the gate, seeing me she became surprised and a little angry too, "brother where have you been for the last one and a half years, dad and mom are so worried about you, they called many times to your company and your company always told that you are busy, how can you be so busy that you don't have time to even talk with your family?" then she hugged me lightly, after that, Hanna drew her attention, looking at Hanna she shouted, "who is she? Don't tell me that you have got married."

"No, it is not like that," I replied to my sister, "she is just my friend, her name is Hanna"

"Now can I come inside?" I asked my sister bantering a bit.

"Yeah bro, come in," and while looking at Hanna she said, "you too, come inside," while Hanna and I were walking inside my home just behind my sister she called for mother and father,

"Mom and dad, its brother, Ishan, he has come, along with his girlfriend, I think," and she winked at me while saying so. Hanna also smiled at it, seeing this my sister remarked, "oh, this might be true," then she whispered in my ear, "by the way she is pretty, bro" and she blushed once again after saying so.

I had reached the hall of my home till now, Hanna was right behind me, after listening to the voice of my sister, father and mother came out from their room.

"Oh, son," father said with a crackling voice, "why were you not calling back, how come you can be so busy in your work that you forgot to talk with your family, is it the right thing to do, son, tell me. Your mom was worrying so much she even became ill while worrying about you,"

"I am sorry dad, I won't do this ever again, I was just trying to learn how to do business of diamonds and so far, I have learned only this, there is cutthroat competition in the business world and to survive for a newcomer is only a fluke," I had few drops of tears in my eyes.

"Oh, my poor boy," said my father in a faint voice and hugged me. My mother also hugged me and said, "now promise me you will not go again there and will work in our sweet shop, running sweet shop is also a good business, you should not feel inferior to anyone," while saying so she had tears in her eyes, I wiped her tears and said, "I promise mom, I will never leave you again, I did not like that place anyway, that place is filled with greedy people. I will never go there." Mom hugged once again. Then she looked at Hanna and asked me,

"Who is she? She looks, a foreigner."

"She is my friend, her name is Hanna, she had come here to visit various places of Delhi. She was not able to get a hotel, so I told her to come to my home. After visiting various places in Delhi, she will leave to her house in goa," I replied.

"Hello, aunty and hello uncle," Hanna said

"Hello, Hanna" replied both my mom and dad.

"Both of you get fresh than have some food," said my father.

After getting ourselves fresh we had food, with the whole family after so long time.

***

It was almost 8 PM. I along with Hanna was watching television in the guest room. My father was also sitting beside us.

"So are you ready to take full responsibly for our sweet shop, after all, your adventure of running a business of diamonds seems to have given no result," said my father.

"Oh dad," I replied in a bit of frustration, "don't taunt me, not everyone gets successful in establishing a new business, what if I got flopped ?"

"All right son, I was just kidding. By the way, get ready you will handle shop from tomorrow."

"Sure dad," I replied.

"I am leaving to my room, after watching television, get your friend to rest in Roshni room, ok"

"Ok, dad," I once again replied while watching TV. My father left the guest room and went to his room. Hanna was eagerly waiting for this so that she could talk with me without restrictions.

"So," she gazed at me anxiously and said, "you are planning to stay in your world, what about my world. Won't you help our people? You have promised me Ishaan. How can you do this after promising me?" she had few tears streaming on her cheeks.

"I know I promised you but try to understand Hanna, I am the only son of my parent, and how can I abandon my parent. If something happens to me in your world who will look after my parents. I have also a sister and my parents are worried about getting her married. Tell me how can I abdicate my responsibility toward my family?" I replied.

"Nothing will happen to you," said Hanna with an almost pleading look on her face, "I can promise this, after all, you are the kind-hearted hero. Please think about it. Please Ishaan;" she was almost on the verge of crying. Her voice was crackling.

"All right, all right please don't cry please give me some time to think about it," I asked.

"Ok," she replied while wiping her tears.

After some time, my sister came there and took Hanna into her room and I went to my room for sleeping.

***

It was 10 a.m. I was sitting at the counter of my shop. I was looking at Singhania Jewelers', the shop of jewellery in front of our shop. It was filled with customers as usual. Although it was early morning time, the sun was shining as if it has already been afternoon. I was able to hear the tick, tick sound of the wall watch hanging in our shop. My father was reading a newspaper, sitting on the chair beside me. Suddenly a police jeep parked itself in front of our shop. Few constables and one sub-inspector descended from it. Inspector pointed his pistol toward me and shouted,

"Don't move Ishaan, otherwise I will shoot you."

I stood up from my seat and raised my hand in the air. Constables came to me. One of the constables held my collar and the other squeezed my hand and handcuffed me. They both started dragging me. My father tried to stop them, "why are you taking my son like a criminal, what has he done after all?" my father shouted. Sub-inspector came to my father and shouted, "your son is a thief, he has stolen diamonds from the mine of Rocky Bhati along with his girlfriend, another team has gone to your home for searching the diamonds. They will also come here soon after taking diamonds and arresting his girlfriend,"

"No father," I cried, "he is telling lie, she is not my girlfriend and we have not stolen diamond, this is a false accusation of Rocky Bhati, he is trapping me in his deceitful plan," sub-inspector slapped me and said, "oh so Rocky is trapping you now, you stole diamonds and blame Rocky of conspiring against you, take this rascal in the jeep, inside police station I will teach him a lesson."

"Please don't take my son, he is innocent," pleaded my father to the inspector. "Court will decide whether your son is innocent or not," after saying so inspector pushed my father. Seeing this I shouted,

"Inspector don't cross your limit, why are you pushing my father. If you must arrest me then just arrest me. Don't dare to touch my father," I was looking at that inspector with a furious look in my eyes.

"Just throw him inside the jeep, what are you looking at," the inspector shouted at the constables. Just then another jeep came there, from that jeep few constables alighted, Hanna was also in that jeep and she was also handcuffed. I looked at her and she while looking at me shouted,

"Ishaan, why have they arrested me, they are saying that we have stolen diamonds from Rocky, I don't understand this, I do not even know what diamonds are," a lady constable was sitting beside her. That constable asked her to keep quiet.

One constable came to the inspector and handed a small pouch to him and said, "these are the diamonds, I confiscated from the lady, she was telling that it belonged to her, I doubt that these are the same diamonds stolen from the mines of Rocky Bhati,"

"Very well," replied the inspector, then he turned toward me, "so what will you say now, it seems your accomplice has been caught red-handed," then he shouted once again, "put this thief inside the jeep," constables pushed me inside the jeep.

Hanna and I were taken to jail and were put in the same cell. Hanna and I sat on the floor of the cell. Hanna looked devastated. She was extremely anguished. She looked at me and said,

"I don't understand why they have put us into jail," she was very anxious, "we will have to go to my realm and save the realm from that black-cloaked devil, and now we have got stuck here in your world without any power, I can understand why your world doesn't have any control on fundamental forces of nature, your world has so much evilness in it, god must have revoked this control, no one listens to others here. I was stating that those are the currency of my world, yet that man accused me of stealing those currencies from Rocky, why the hell

I would do that? Tell me Ishaan," she was now visibly frustrated. I could feel that. Yeah, it's true in the earthly realm eager is the main driving force for a man, and I also thought that it might be true what she had said, after all seeing all the devious things a man does God must have thought human beings not worthy to have the control of fundamental forces of nature.

I gazed at Hanna and said, "don't worry Hanna, we will get some way out of this situation, by the way, those currencies of your world, are called diamonds in our world and they are quite expensive in this world. That's why policemen are thinking that we have stolen those diamonds from Rocky."

"But those are my currencies, how they can snatch those from me," Hanna was angry and then she made a fist and bumped onto the floor of the cell.

As far as I could say almost one hour had passed. The gate of our cell opened. It was dark inside the cell. The only light was coming from that gate. As the light was coming from behind the face of the person who stood at the opened gate of the cell was not visible clearly. He came near us. Now the face was visible. He was Rocky Bhati. He was a somewhat stout man with a height of around 7 feet and looked quite muscular. His face was almost square and there was a deep dark circle all around his eyes. His lips were very fat just like his two fat biceps. He came near us and smirked.

"How are you Mr Ishaan and Miss Hanna, ha ha ha," he laughed while looking at us.

"Sir," I said, "we have not stolen your diamonds, those diamonds belong to us if we tell from where we got those diamonds you will not be able to believe us, please sir, try to understand we have not stolen your diamonds,"

"Yes, sir," Hanna also said, "those are currencies of my world, those are not diamonds of your world,"

"Ha, Ha, Ha," laughed Rocky after listening to our pleading, then he said "I know this don't worry. I made the complaint so that both of may get stuck here and I could make my plunder of that realm of Hanna, Ha, Ha, Ha,"

I was puzzled listening to this and so was Hanna.

"So, you know that I am from another realm," asked Hanna.

"Yeah, I know that," replied Rocky "and both of you will rot in this cell while I conquer the other realm, I will be God of that Real, ha ha ha, only this Ishaan has been prophesied to stop me, and now he is stuck in this earthly realm, he cannot use all the power other realms here."

"I did not understand what you want to say?" I asked.

"Well," he replied, "now both of you cannot stop me then I must say the truth, the mind-boggling truth, and get ready to crumble under your feet, ha, ha, ha," he laughed once again cunningly.

I was becoming frustrated with all his blabbering, "oh please cut the crap and say directly what do you want to say, I am feeling sleepy with your boring monologue, just say what do you want to say," I shouted.

"Well," he said "I am your black-cloaked devil, ha, ha, ha,"

Hanna and I become paralyzed with fear listening to this. After saying so he left the cell. We were staring at each other.

CHAPTER 9: ASTRAL BODY

Hanna and I were looking at each other ominously, "oh god," I said, "so he is black-cloaked devil, Rocky Bhati of my world is the villain of your world, how can this be possible, as you told me only kind-hearted guy can cross the wishing well."

"I don't know, we can get an answer from that book of wishing well and the king is in the possession of that book. First, we will have to go to my realm if we want to find answers in that book, how can we go there now?" she closed her eyes and took a deep breath then she suddenly gazed at me and said, "well the first question is how we came here, I have read somewhere that a fifth level citizen can open an inter-dimensional portal to a place where he has already visited. And you are a fifth level citizen, I think you are slowly accessing your fifth level abilities and you made that portal accidentally to save both of us,"

"I don't know," I replied, "that might be the case, but in my world, we cannot access control over fundamental forces of nature. It might be that I accidentally opened a portal to my world but here I can't make that happen again."

"At least you should try," she stared at me, "who knows you might succeed?"

"Well, how can I try, in this world, I cannot access my life energy just like you can't access yours. Tell me how can I try?"

"I don't know," she said frustratingly, "but there is no other way, only you can take us to my realm, you must try."

"All right, let me see if I can access my life energy in this realm also or not," I replied. Then I sat in thunderbolt position. I tried to concentrate all my thought on my life energy to access it. But it was in vain. After trying for some time, I got tired and laid down on the floor of the cell.

"I am too tired to concentrate, I am taking nap now," I said.

"Yeah," she replied, "take rest, after some time, do try again," and she also laid down beside me to take rest.

I closed my eyes. Within a snap of seconds, I was in a dream-like state. After a few more seconds, I was in a dream. I was sitting on a bench in a park. It was like any ordinary park in Delhi. People were exercising, jogging and talking to each other. It was perhaps morning time. Just then, white smog appeared all around. All those people start escaping from there turning into smoke. A cloud of black smoke was coming to the park from the sky. Within a few seconds, it collided with the grass of the park. Then it raised to the height of a normal guy and started slowly turning into a man. Firstly, all internal organs appeared in the air, then bones, then skin, and then a black mist engrossed the whole of the body. Soon it was pretty much clear. He was the black-cloaked guy. Or in other words, he was Rocky. I think he was using his power of dream casting. He had perhaps entered my dream to kill me. He appeared fully in his black-cloaked attire in front of me. He came closer to me.

"Ha, ha, ha," his laugh was extremely acrimonious and felt very real then he said, "you have done the last mistake of your life. you will die with my hand. I think you don't know that I can kill anyone in his dream. Yet you slept, so sad for you,"

"Well," I asked in apprehension, "if you going to kill me then can you tell me how you enter the other realm. Because the wishing well is closed for travel the night I entered through that path."

"Well, well," he replied, "do you think that I will tell you my secret, even in your dream I will not tell you my secret," then he stopped momentarily and laughed once again, "I forgot, it's your dream, ha, ha, ha, so funny," then he smirked. He held his hand in front of his chest and the same diamond sword appeared.

"Now get ready to die, last time that chief of defence department saved your life, but this time who will save you, ha, ha, ha."

After saying so he pounced toward me and swung the sword. I trusted myself backwards to escape from his attack.

"Ha, ha, ha, whatever you do you will not live this time," he shouted and once again came flying toward me. I was seeing the end of me at that moment, but the death time of mine was not near me yet. Rocky's sword was about to hit me but just at that moment a white mist collided with me from the left side, and it throttled me away from the line of attack of the sword. I staggered on the ground and with difficulty, I got up. That white mist also settled beside me and soon it converted into a man, it was the king, King Justin Edgar. I gazed at him in surprise. He was panting and I was also gasping. Then I remembered it was my dream why I was gasping. Anyway, I looked at the king, the king looked at me and winked at me then he said,

"Ishan, you wait here I will deal with that black-cloaked devil now," the king roared and pounced toward Rocky with his diamond sword. There ensued a deadly fight between two-level fifth citizens in my dream. A few minutes passed, both were fighting on almost equal footing, it seemed they have almost equal powers. I thought that's why the king cannot defeat that black-cloaked guy and there needed a hero to be summoned from another realm having a pure heart.

After fighting for a few minutes. Black cloaked devil backtracked and flew away while saying, "Ishaan, I will see you some other time, this time also you were lucky,"

King came to me and asked "Ishaan, how are you I am really worried about you, some of my spies said that black-cloaked devil attacked you while you were coming toward me, then you and Hanna disappeared in mid-air, I started searching for you using my dream searching power, just the way black-cloaked guy has dream casting power, I have dream searching power, although I cannot kill anyone like dream caster, but I can save anyone including myself from a dream caster and search dream of anyone. Now tell me where you are,"

"I am stuck in my world, I think I accidentally opened a portal to my world when the black-cloaked guy was attacking me, but in my world, I cannot access my life energy so I cannot open portal, there. And also, I came to know about the true identity of the black-cloaked

guy. He is from my world. His name is Rocky Bhati."

King became anxious listening to this, "oh I see,

that's why he appears in our world momentarily and now

I understood why he is after you so badly."

"I did not get it what do you want to say," I

asked.

"Well Ishaan," he replied, "as you already know

that any person from your world can not enter to our

world unless he has a pure heart and that too through

wishing well, and about that chief has told me that, the

wishing well has been closed permanently the day you

entered our world. But there is another way to enter our

world for those evil people whose hearts are not pure.

And for any person of our world who got stuck into your

world and for good-hearted people like you there is a

simple way,"

"It means Rocky knows the way to enter your

realm," I asked.

"Yes Ishaan, he knows," the king replied, "as his

heart is not pure so his body cannot enter our realm, but

his astral form can enter into our realm, but an astral form into another realm cannot stay for much longer that's why he appears in my realm for some time only. I think there must have been some incident with him due to that he is stuck in the earthly realm of yours."

"Oh," I replied, "I understood now so he can enter your realm as astral form, but what is astral form, I have not learned it yet and can I also use my power using the astral form in my realm?"

"Yes," replied the king, "if you separate the astral form of you from your body then you can use life energy in the earthly realm also using your astral body then you can create a portal to my world and enter into it, after all, you are a fifth level citizen you can do it."

"But" I replied, "I don't know how to separate astral form and also I don't know how to create the portal."

"You know everything Ishaan, after all, you are a kind-hearted hero," the king said.

"I have a few more questions, as Hanna told me that any person from force realm if entering my realm will lose all his life energy but when Hanna entered with me she didn't lose it, then how could the chief have lost her life energy?" I asked.

"Well, about losing life energy, it's not true, it was just hypothesised by the medical staff of defence department as I did not oppose this hypothesis they thought it to be true. I also thought that this will act as an inhibitor for anyone who wishes to cross to your realm. And about the chief, she lost her life energy because I had given her my dream searching and portal opening power momentarily. That's why she was able to enter your dream. Only citizens of level five can make an inter-dimensional portal. But it requires great learning. Keep in mind it's our little secret So I think you have answers to your questions," the king said while he was transforming into the mist, "I have complete faith in you Ishaan, now get up use your astral body to control fundamental forces of nature, make a portal and come to my castle, we will have to make a plan to defeat that Rocky or black-cloaked guy whatever you call him, now hurry up." After saying so king vanished from my dream.

I woke up gasping from my dream. Hanna also became worried and got up

"What happened are you alright?" she asked.

"Rocky tried to attack me using his power dream caster," I replied. She was frightened to the core listening to this, "are you alright now, did he hurt you?"

"I'm all right, you don't need to worry about me, king saved me," I replied.

"King?" she asked curiously, "does king also have the power of dream casting?"

"No," I replied, "he has the power of dream searching, his spies had told him about our encounter with the black-cloaked devil, so he was searching me using his dream searching power. Luckily he found me in time."

"Thank god," sighed Hanna, "what else king told you?"

"He said," I replied, "rocky is using the astral form to enter in your realm, and he told me that I can also access my life energy using the astral form, but I don't know how to separate astral form from my body."

"I have learned about the astral form," Hanna replied, "using the astral form we can control the fundamental forces of nature in any realm, in your realm too. But only level five or above citizens can access astral form, so now only you can save us,"

"That is alright but," I said, "how to separate the astral form from the physical body, can you tell me?"

"I also don't know," she replied while making an innocent face. Then a few seconds later she said, "you are a level fifth citizen, think something, as only level fifth citizens can do this, they don't even need to learn about it. It is in their blood."

"All right," I replied, "let me try to again concentrate my thought toward my astral body this time." I once again sat in thunderbolt position and this time I concentrated all my energy on my soul, I thought the soul might be an astral form of the body after all. After a few minutes, it seemed everything around me was becoming blurred. After some more seconds passed and it seemed everything shifted sharply toward left for about a few feet. Everything was glowing now as I opened my eyes. A surge of life energy I was able to feel within me. I looked toward my hands and my feet and my body it was all glowing. It was feeling so light as if I had lost all my weight. And my feet were not touching the grounds, I was hovering in the air. I could see every force of nature distinctively now. I was seeing the space-time curve all around me. I was seeing the curving effects of all mass possessing objects around me on this space-time curve resulting in the production of illusion, which is called gravitational force, oh my god, what an illusion is this which is called gravitational force. I was feeling all the neutral charges in every matter. How splendidly negative and positive electrical charges balance each other inside every visible and invisible matter of the universe. I was seeing the spins of those electrons and protons; I was seeing the magnetism produced by those spinning charges. I was also feeling the weak nuclear forces. They are so magnificent forces, extremely powerful in extremely small dimensions that is, within the nucleus of those tiny atoms. I was feeling the presence of nuclear forces the first time. I was feeling as if I could rearrange those nucleons at my will and change the atoms from within. I was feeling the power to create any atoms from the given atoms. My strong urges to diamonds overpowered my senses and within a few splashes of time, I converted some of the dirt fallen on the floor into the most high-quality diamonds available.

"Ishan are you all right, why don't you say something," was the voice I heard when I was living all these dream-like states.

"Ishaan are you listening to me," Hanna shouted to full of her voice.

I looked at Hanna, she was also glowing. I was able to see all the electrical and chemical reactions going inside her boy. Her dopamine level in the brain was at a considerably higher level. Then beside her, I saw my body sitting on the ground. Then I became confused seeing my own body. After a few more seconds, I realized that I was in my astral body now and in the astral body I was feeling all the fundamental forces of nature. Hanna came slowly toward me.

"So, Ishaan, calm down. I think this is your first out of body experience in astral form so you will need some time to adjust to it, now please focus on me and my voice and try to calm down yourself," she tried to calm me and gazed toward me in a gentle way and with her evergreen blush. I was trying to calm myself now, I looked at the blushing face of Hanna. Her face was becoming more beautiful for me as I was able to see all the sparkling going on behind the skin of her face, all the nerve endings sending and receiving stimuli, all the lovely creations of nature, in other words. My astral body now came at the level of Hanna, she tried to touch my hand and likewise, I tried to touch her hand, but her hands passed through mine like my hand was made of fog. It just pierced through it.

"So, in astral form, I can't touch you," I said so and smiled. She also smiled and then I remembered what the king had said to me.

"Hanna," I said, "King told me that Rocky enters the other realm in the astral body, now I understood why he needs the body of Nathan's brother because in astral form one cannot touch anything or may be one cannot harm anybody, I don't know but I feel so,"

"First let's go to my realm and visit the king, then we will try to find more things about Rocky and Nathan and his brother, try to make a portal to my world, see if you can do it or not." Said Hanna. I looked at her and nodded my hand in affirmatively while closing my both eyes simultaneously.

"All right, here I try to create a portal," I said and, in my mind, I was trying to vividly remember any place of Hanna's realm that would have a strong impression on my memory. The strongest impression on my memory was perhaps made by the garden, where the wishing well was situated. The image inside my memory was steadily making now a homeomorphic relation with the real special entity around the wishing well garden. A small portal appeared in front of me, and it engulfed me, Hann and my body into Hanna's realm. We appeared near the wishing well garden. It was crowded with people as usual. A young lady just then threw a diamond and started making her wishes, "Oh greatest wishing well, please grant me my wish, please search most handsome and most powerful prince for me,"

"Typical wish of any girl," I said while I was looking at her. Then I turned my gaze to Hanna. She was also smiling.

"Now, you can enter in your body, Ishaan. We have reached in my realm," said Hanna with a smile. I entered my body and the heaviness of bodily mass I was feeling that again.

"It felt so weightless in astral form, I will use the astral form more and more now," I spoke.

"Now," said Hanna, "we must go to the king and ask him about the wishing well book, what could have happened to your friend Aditya and many other questions. I think king know a lot of things."

"I also think so," I replied, "let's go."

CHAPTER 10: ARTIFICIAL

INTELLIGENT CONTRIVANCE

Hanna and I entered the king's castle. I used the royal entry pass given to me by the king himself, so no one stopped us on the way. We entered the king's chamber. He was busy in day-to-day administrative work, seeing me he and his ministers stopped. King looked to me and then toward his ministers and ordered in loud voice.

"Let me talk with the kind-hearted hero, Ishaan, all of you may leave now," everyone left the chamber. Hanna and I sat down on chairs beside the round table. King was sitting on the opposite side.

"Hello, your highness," I said. "I hope I have not disturbed you."

"Certainly not, Ishaan, I was just having day to day administrative discussions with my ministers, nothing important," then he looked toward Hanna and further said, "so Miss Hanna, how are you fairing as assistant of kindhearted hero?"

"It's my honour to severe kindhearted hero, sir. I am grateful to you as you bestowed on me such honour," replied Hanna.

"Your highness," I said then, "I have some questions regarding black-cloaked guy and about wishing well book, in headquarter I came to know that it was issued to you,"

"Yes," replied the king, "the wishing well book was issued to me. I got issued this book so that I could close the wishing well for the entry of anyone from the earthly realm, but I am happy that before the closure of that path you were able to cross here. Chief told me just after when I had initiated the closure of wishing well forever that she had discovered a kindhearted hero that is you, so I ordered her to bring you into this world as early as possible but due to that she had to lose her all life energy but thankfully she is recovering very well."

"I beg your pardon sir, but I didn't get your point," I asked with a bewildered expression and squinting at the king, "why did you stop the passage?"

"When I was reading the wishing well book I came to know about a disturbing revelation in the book," King became grim while saying so. Hanna was also staring at king with a thoughtful look on her face.

"What type of revelation, sir?" I queried.

"well," replied the king after clearing his throat, "it was revealed in the book that only kind-hearted hero can pass through wishing well and enter into our realm safely and if any other guy whose heart is not kind will try to pass through the wishing well will be instantly transported to the dark world, and there by to the dark king, the book mentions perhaps black-cloaked devil as the dark king, although I am not sure about it and he is Rocky Bhati of your world, as you told me in your dream, then that guy can easily be converted to Apator, a soulless creature. I investigated about it and came to know that black-cloaked devil possesses an army of Apator now, so I had to close the passage so that no further Apator could be created."

"Oh," I exclaimed after listening to him.

"Anyway, why are you asking about it, Ishaan?" asked the king.

"Sir," I replied with a heavy heart, "before I passed to this realm my friend Aditya fell into that well accidentally and a few days ago when I was searching family book of Adam in record room my friend appeared there as Apator, now I understood how he became Apator," after saying so I became upset and few drops of tear rolled over my cheek, "he is my best friend, I must save him. Do you know sir, how to save an Apator?"

"That's heartbreaking as," replied the king "once a person becomes Apator he cannot be saved, I am sorry to hear about your friend, I have condolence for your friend, we can do nothing about him,"

I became extremely angry listening that, "I will not spare Rocky, he snatched my only best friend from me, and he will pay a heavy price for this,"

"But how we will fight him," said the king, "I am almost equally powerful as that of the black-cloaked devil, I cannot defeat him, and you have to learn more before you will be able to defeat him, I will advise you to complete your master degree, till than I will do more research on him,"

"All right sir, but," I replied, "one more thing, I came to know about Rocky,"

"Well, I am listening, tell me," asked the king.

"Sir," I replied, "Rocky comes to this realm as an astral body, I had told you this already but I came to know that as an astral body he cannot touch anything in this world that's why he needed a body. I came to know whose body he is using, he is using the body of brother of Nathan Adam, my roommate in the hostel."

"Oh, Nathan Adams," replied the king, "I will investigate about it also, you first complete your master degree, Ishaan."

"All right sir, then may I have your permission to leave sir,"

"You may leave," replied the king. Hanna and I left the castle. I continued my master's degree course while having a close eye on the activities of Nathan Adam.

***

It was the time of the morning. Isabel and I were looking at our results on the notice board. The first year was completed and we had given exams. Exams consisted of 60% practical and 40% theory. In the theoretical department, I was average but in the practical department, I was above exceptional. I had scored the highest overall marks. I was placed at rank one and Isabel was placed at rank second. Kira Calhoun, who did not like the low background of Isabel was placed at third so he was visibly furious.

"Wow, congratulation Ishaan you topped the class," said Isabel with blush and excitement.

"Thanks, congratulations to you also, after all, you also secured the second position," and while peeking at Kira I said further, "some people must be getting jealous of you more now," then we both giggled. Kira became more furious and left.

"So, you will have to give me a treat now," said Isabel while smiling.

"Yeah sure," I replied.

"Excuse me, Ishan," it was the voice of the personal assistant of the principal, Mrs Gloria Parker.

"Yes, Mrs Parker," I turned to her.

"Principal Sir wants to see you in his office," she said and left.

"Okay then I should go to the principal office, will see you afterwards okay," I told Isabel.

"Okay," she replied with a blush.

I went toward the principal office. I opened the gate, "May I come in sir, did you call me?" I asked.

"Yes Ishaan, come in, take your seat," said the principal. I entered the office and seated myself in the visitor's chair.

"So, Ishaan, how was your first year." He asked.

"It was fun," I replied, "I learned a lot of things about this realm. I learned how to control gravitational force, how to control electric and magnetic forces and even now I can control weak nuclear force, although that is a bit of long story how I was able to control weak nuclear forces,"

"I know that," replied the principal with a slight smile on his face. I became a little mystified hearing this. "You know?" I asked.

"Yes, I know, His highness, the king told me about your quick tour to your earthly realm, and how you activated your Astral body and returned to our realm. Now as the astral body can only be activated by the highest degree of the fifth level user, so I think you are now ready to learn fifth level power utilization."

"I am ready?" I pronounced to him.

"Yes, you are ready. But no one in this world can tell you about that and no one can teach you fifth level stuff and more information about this world and many other things," replied the principal.

"If no one can teach me then how will I learn about fifth level things?" I asked with surprise. The principal laughed a bit listening to this and then he replied.

"I mean no human can teach you this, fifth level stuff is taught to selected one only and you are third after the king, and that black-cloaked guy, we all have mysteriously forgotten his real name, anyway, I was stating that you are third after those two to have the fifth level. Only a few people in billion possess the fifth level of power and they are taught by special artificial intelligent contrivance. That machine is in the fifth level class. You must have seen that class. I have never seen it because it is covered by a special force field which can be crossed by only fifth lever citizen and I am at only level three as you know,"

"All right, so I will have to go myself in that fifth level class," I asked.

"Yes, Ishaan," the principal replied while giving me a small diamond-shaped cube, "take this key. This will open the gate to fifth level class, and also before entering into the field which is covering special artificial intelligent contrivance, do talk with the king, as per his instruction given to me, I am saying this,"

"Ok sir," I said, and I took the diamond cube. Now I became a little curious that why important things in this world were made of diamonds? Like the currency of there was made of diamonds, the sword by which Rocky attacked me in my dream was made of diamond, the pass given to me by the king was also made of diamond and this key to fifth level class is also made of diamond.

"If you don't mind, can I ask you something sir," I asked principal

"Sure, ask anything Ishaan," he replied,

"Sir, why most of the important things in this world are made of diamond?" I asked.

"Diamond," he repeated it strangely. Then I remembered that in my world it is called diamond not here.

"Sir, I mean this precious stone," showing him the key I said, "this is called 'diamond' in my world and it's very precious in my world but in your world, it has many different uses,"

"Oh, so it is called 'diamond' in your world," he replied, "even I don't know about this, I only know that only fifth level users know about this element. Throughout the kingdom, this element is provided by the king's castle only. Only the king can answer you regarding this, and I think the king will answer your questions because you are also fifth level citizen just like the king himself,"

"All right sir, I will contact the king before going to fifth level class, now I will take my leave," I said and left the office of the principal.

***

Isabel was sipping her beverage 'arometa', this was one of its kind of beverage of that realm. It was made of dried fruit 'arom' found in that realm having taste almost like cocoa powder of earthly realm. I was also sitting beside her and sipping the same beverage.

"So," she said while sipping the 'arometa', "you will now enter the fifth level classroom,"

"Yeah, but before that, I will have to talk to the king regarding diamonds, the principal told me all the diamonds comes from the castle and only fifth level citizen can know about diamonds,"

She smiled a bit and looked at me, "so, can I enter in fifth level class also with you?"

"I don't think so, only fifth level are allowed to enter there. Even principle cannot enter." I replied.

"Seriously," she was surprised.

"Yeah," I replied while gulping my 'arometa'.

***

I was waiting for the king, in the visitor hall of the king's castle. I had come to visit king before entering the fifth level class.

"Your highness," I said when I saw the king entering the visitor hall.

"What's going Ishaan, how's your study going in the academy, I heard that you topped the class, that's very nice. Now I am sure that you will defeat the black-cloaked devil." He asked while entering the hall. "Take your seat and be comfortable young boy,"

"Thank you, sir," I replied while sitting on a chair placed beside the table. King also sat on the centre chair of the table. It was a huge table having more than 50 chairs all around it.

"I am fine sir, I have to ask you something that's why I came here," I asked the king.

"What do you want to ask Ishaan?" asked the king.

"Sir," I responded, "I want to ask about diamonds, I mean the currency of your world and more information about your world."

"I can understand your curiosity Ishaan," said the king, "but I am not authorized to answer your questions, you will find all your answers in that fifth level class only. I also found my answer there only and in that class, I was given an oath that I will not divulge the secrets of this world and the secrets of fifth level power to anyone. Any fifth level citizen will find his answers by himself in that class,"

"In that case," I replied, "I will enter fifth level class soon,"

"That will be great," replied the king. After that, I left for the academy.

***

I was standing near the gate of the fifth level class. It was a huge gate with splendid designs made of pure diamonds covering all over it. I took the diamond key of that class from my pocket. There was a keyhole of almost similar shape as that of the diamond key in the gate. I inserted the key there. The gate opened. But just behind the gate, there was an invisible boundary made of some kind of force field. There was something written over it. I read it.

"Be careful passer-by, this is the gate for only level fifth citizen. If you are not a level fifth citizen, you must return immediately otherwise your soul will be trapped into the well of flame for eternity. There is no escape from that well of flame. Be careful passer-by,"

I entered through that boundary slowly. As I entered inside, I saw there was a sphere in the middle. It was a hall, quite a big one and there was nothing else except that sphere. The sphere was hovering over the floor, it was in the air. It was shining and there was no other light source in the hall. It appeared that there was some sort of cyclone trapped inside the sphere. I went near the sphere.

"Hello, fifth level user, after so long time I am visited by another fifth level user, I hope you are not useless like the last one. The last fifth level user was complete trash. I don't know how he was able to enter this world, by the way, I am the sphere of eternity, and I am also known as an artificial intelligent contrivance. I guide and examine fifth level users in this world. What's your name? You can ask me anything. Just ask. I will clear all your doubts," sphere was talking to me.

"Well, my name is Ishaan and yeah I have many questions but what you were telling about the last fifth level user?" I asked.

"About that, you will know only after passing my test but first I will tell you everything about this world and after that if you still have any questions you can ask. Then you will have to pass my test. Only after passing my test, you will be able to use fifth level power. It will be manifested as secret power that will be known only after completion of the test," said the sphere.

"All right," I replied, "tell me about this world,"

"Very well," replied the sphere, "now listen carefully, this is the world of fundamental forces. It is called the force realm. There are infinite realms. They all were created after the big bang. In your realm, that is the earthly realm all these realms are called parallel universes."

"Oh, I sea," I replied, "so the theory of the parallel universes is correct,"

"Yes, of course," replied the sphere, "that theory is correct but only partially. There indeed exists infinite parallel universes, but they are not identical. Fundamental forces of nature behave differently in different universes. In your earthly universe, fundamental forces are absolute rulers, no one can control fundamental forces. Humans are just slaves of fundamental forces."

"What! We are a slave?" I said grimly.

"Yes, my dear Ishaan. In the earthly realm, humans are just slaves of these fundamental forces. They cannot control these fundamental forces at all. Fundamental forces control humanity and all type of matter in the earthly realm. Some great brains like those of Einstein and newton have tried to understand how some of these fundamental forces work but still, they were not able to understand completely. And most of the other human beings of your world have just surrendered themselves to the will of forces of nature."

"I did not understand what you want to say?" I asked.

"I am saying that most people of the earthly realm have submitted themselves to fundamental forces and given them the work of some kind of god, an entity of mere imagination of earthly human being. God is nothing but a fragment of imagination of the weak shivering mind of the earthly human being." Replied the sphere.

"So," I asked, "you are saying that there exists no god?"

"Yes," sphere replied, "there exists no god. In the earthly realm, a human cannot control fundamental forces, so they consider the work of fundamental forces as the work of God. These fundamental forces work on a large scale. They don't even bother about human beings. The human being came into existence just due to pure coincidences."

"What type of coincident?" I murmured in a faint voice.

"Yes, Ishaan," replied the sphere, "pure coincident, anyway leave that I will tell you in detail about that some other time. Now is the time for telling you other things and of course testing you for your capabilities and your pureness of heart? You will have to prove now that your heart is pure, or you are just pretending to have pure heart,"

"Well, I don't know about that myself either, first tell me more about this force realm," I replied.

"This is force realm. One of the parallel universes." Replied the sphere, "this is a fifth-dimensional realm. Your earth is a fourth-dimensional realm. In this realm, fundamental forces of nature can be controlled using life forces. Life forces are present in the fifth dimension of this realm."

"Fifth dimension!" I repeated with surprise.

"Yes, the fifth dimension," replied the sphere, "only fifth level citizens or citizens having a level above than fifth can access the fifth dimension. That is why they have almost infinite life energy. All other human gets their life energy from the leaked life energy from the fifth dimension. And any fifth level citizen can access a pocket of the fifth dimension and use that as a storage house and for anything else. That you will learn after completing the test. For now, more about the force realm and other realms. As I have already told you that there exist parallel realms but only a few of them are habitable and other realm contains only darkness as opposed to your earthly parallel universe theory. The earthly parallel universe theory conjectures other universes to be a copy of each other but that is not true at all. Only a few parallel universes have life forms. Because fundamental forces of each parallel universe behave differently that's why only a few of them possess the qualities which allow life forms to exist. And in most parallel universes, fundamental forces do not allow any life forms to exist. Till now I have been able to discover only two other parallel universes other than this force realm where life form exists. One is your earthly realm and the other is the realm of adventure. The realm of adventure is sixth-dimensional and, in that realm, you will be tested for whether you have a pure heart or not. Now get ready for your test. Before I send you in that realm you can ask any question which might be in your mind,"

"Yes," I replied, "I have many questions,"

CHAPTER 11: REALM OF ADVENTURE

"Ask Ishaan, what you want to ask?" spoke the sphere.

"I want to know about diamonds, why diamonds are so prevalent in this force realm?" I asked.

"About that, you will come to know after test in the realm of adventure." Replied the sphere.

"It seems," I said, "most of my answers will be found only after the test. I think I am ready for the test now."

"That's the spirit," said the sphere, "now I am sending you in the realm of adventure. All the best for the test." When the sphere said so few light rays emerged from it and met at a point in the air beside it. There appeared another sphere, initially small and then grew bigger just like a portal that was created by me to enter force realm from the earthly realm. That sphere engulfed me into it. For a few seconds, it felt that I was floating amongst the stars. Then it felt I was being sucked into a black hole. A giant black hole was pulling me toward it. I became frightened. But then I heard the voice of the sphere of eternity.

"Don't fear, you will not be engulfed into the black hole, it is just visual of other universes on the way toward the realm of adventure."

After a few seconds, I crossed the black hole and still I was flying across countless stars. I was enveloped by the sphere. It was perhaps protecting me in this journey.

A few more seconds and a strange planet appeared before me. Its star was of the shape of oval rather than round like our sun. I was flying into the planet now. I crossed clouds having all the sparkling colour I could ever imagine. Then I slowly touched the ground there. I was surrounded by thick fog now. It was harder to see beyond a few yards. After one- or two minutes fog started disappearing and I was able to see a lush green jungle. It had tall trees with lots of branches. Sunlight was permeating through them giving a smoothening warm feeling near the ground. I was standing on a path made of yellow and find fragments of unknown types of rock. As I was wondering what I should do now, I heard steps closing in from behind. Firstly, I tried to analyze whether I can control or not the fundamental forces of nature in this world. But it was a failed exercise as I was not feeling any flow of fundamental forces around me. I quickly turned around to see who was making that sound of stepping. I was seeing a few remnants of white fog there as if someone were there and just disappeared while I turned to him. I felt that someone was once again behind me. I once again turned and now I was seeing myself in front of me.

"Hello, sir," my clone said while giving awkward smile to me. I stayed silent for a few seconds.

"Sorry to disturb you, sir, in this world we are formless. We do not have any form. We are just like a transparent matter ball, which could change its shape. So, I thought to interact with you it would be nice if I seem to appear just like you,"

"All right," I replied, "So can you show me your real form?"

"Yeah, sure," he said and turned into a floating mess of uneven round shape which was somewhat translucent. Then he once again turned into my façade. "Sir, will you come with me? My leader wants to meet you. He saw your entry into our world through his all-seeing eyes. He is very powerful. He can see everything that is happening in this world at a given moment."

"Hmm," I looked at him, "you did not tell me about your name by the way."

"Sir, we do not have names. Only our leader has a name. His name is the one" he replied. "Please follow me, sir."

"All right," I replied and followed him. We went on a square platform. The platform started raising upward and was now flying toward a highly raised mountain. There was a grand building almost at the top of the mountain. It had five stories and each of them was extremely high. The main gate was incredibly large. Platform settled itself in front of the main gate. We entered the main gate. Inside the main gate, there was a big hallway and at the end of the hallway, a person with having a similar face as that of mine was sitting on a raised podium, on a grand chair made of silver coloured material. On both sides of the hallway people having my face were standing. We went near the sitting clone of me and the clone who brought me there bowed,

"Your highness, supreme leader, the one, I have fetched our visitor." He said and went toward the side and joined other people standing there.

The one looked toward me with a sceptical look and then said, "so why have you come to our world? What do you want? Have you come here to steal my power?"

"No, your highness. I have not come here to steal your power." I replied stuttering.

"Then tell me, his voice was louder now, "what is the purpose of your visit and from where you have come?"

"Sir," I replied with some apprehension, "I have come from force realm and sphere of eternity has sent me here for some type of test, he did not explain what type of test though."

"Oh," replied the one, "so you are being tested for the worthiness of the fifth level, we are told to do the test on worthy people of force realm to examine whether they are worthy of the fifth level or not. By the way, your test has already begun. And if you fail in this test, you will be banished into the dark world of force realm. Just like the last visitor was banished. I think his name was Rocky, he was extremely greedy of power and now he is rotting in the dark world."

"was Rocky also a fifth level citizen of force realm. How did he enter into the force realm? Was he also kindhearted? I am told that only a Kind-hearted person can enter force realm through wishing well?" I queried.

"I don't know about that. I am here only to test your worthiness and your test is undergoing. Pass the test and return to your realm and ask yourself the sphere of eternity. He knows all the parallel universe. He must know about rocky. At present moment you must focus on passing my test, and I doubt whether you will be able to pass it. If you fail, you will also be banished into the dark world and there you can ask rocky."

"But," I said, "Rocky cannot enter force realm in the physical body. He is banished from there. I don't know why."

"What," he was surprised hearing this, "as far as I know, no one can escape the dark world. Only Apator can escape but becoming Apator is a curse. Apator don't have soul, in other world Apator are only matter aggregated by some forces following the command of the king of the dark world,"

"Is Rocky the king of the dark world?" I asked.

"Of course not," he replied, "he can't be king of the dark world, why are you saying so,"

"Well," I said "I don't know, I just guessed. One of my friends has become Apator. He fell into wishing well and got sucked into the dark world. It might be possible there Rocky converted him into Apator."

The one was now looking toward me and almost staring. He squinted and sighed.

"Well," he replied, "you surely have lots of questions. First, pass your test then in the force realm ask the sphere of eternity. He must know answers to your all questions."

"All right sir," I replied, "but what type of test I will be assessed. Can you tell me at least that?"

"You are already being tested. Just figure it out and pass it. All the best,"
The one along with his throne disappeared. All other clones of mine disappeared as well. The main gate of the hall closed itself. Now there was darkness all around me. I was not able to see anything.

***

I was standing at a crossing. Sun was shining brightly over my head. It was around mid-noon. I looked all around curiously, as I could not remember how I came here, although the roads were all familiar. I remembered it was a crossing nearby my sweet shop.

"Hey Ishan," was the voice that I heard from behind. This voice seemed familiar. I turned and saw the smiling face of Anya Singhania, daughter of the jewellery shop owner, the shop which was opposite to my sweet shop. Although I liked her, I was having a strange feeling seeing her.

"Hi, Anya, what's up?" I replied.

"So, let's go," she said while adjusting her purse over her soldier.

"Where?" I asked hesitantly.

"don't say that you forgot?" she was visibly frustrated now, and few wrinkles appeared over her forehead.

"I am sorry, but I am not remembering where we were planning to go?" I replied.

"Idiot, you forgot. You told me to meet you today here, then we will go to watch a movie," she said.

"I am kidding, don't be angry. I remember," said I although I had no clue how I reached that crossing. I was feeling some type of amnesia. I could not remember any prior incidents. The last thing I could remember was that I, along with my friend Aditya Rana, were planning to start a diamond company together.

I was feeling a dreamlike state. Although I was watching a movie in the theatre, I could not focus on the movie. At about 9 pm I reached home.

***

After having dinner, I was watching TV. My father came there and sat beside me.

"Ishan, where were you after midday and you came home so late today?" asked my father.

"I was with my friend Aditya, we watched a movie and walked for a while at the nearby park."

"Okey," said he, then after a few seconds of pause further he continued.

"Son, now you have taken full responsibility of our shop, you should get married."

My gaze shifted to my father's face after hearing these words.

"Papa, I need some time to think about marriage. It's too soon. First, we have to think about the wedding of Roshni," I replied exasperatingly.

"Are you alright son?" asked my father after few seconds of pause.

"I am alright, why are you asking so?"

"Because Roshni has been married 3 months ago, it seems you forgot, how this can be? Are you really alright, you seem different person than yesterday? Yesterday you were saying about getting married yourself and you told me that you like Anya. What happened to you?"

I was shocked hearing this. I felt like I was at some other place. This was not my home. But I was not able to remember anything. Every desire of heart seems to be fulfilled in this new reality of which I was not sure part of.

"No papa, there is nothing to worry about. I am having headache little bit. Nothing else" I replied.

"All right then go and sleep in your room. Tomorrow I will talk to father of Anya, good night."

"Good night," I said and left for my room.

***

I was sitting at the counter of my sweet shop. It was about 11 am. A huge crowd of customers were standing in a queue in front of my shop for buying sweets as if my shop has become super famous overnight. Workers were busy. We had hired a cashier also although I was not able to remember when we hired him. I was seeing posts on social media on my phone about my shop.

"Good morning, Ishan," it was the voice of Anya. I looked at her she was standing in front of the counter and was in ecstasy and blush all over her face.

"Good morning," I replied. "You seem very happy today, what happened?"

"Guess," she chuckled.

"Tell me please," I asked while making an annoyed facial expression.

"My father said yes," she chuckled once again after saying so.

I looked at her in a shocked visage.

"I did not understand, what do you want to say," I asked.

"Idiot, my father said yes to the proposal of our marriage," she replied, "I am very happy, we are going to get married next month, isn't this great Ishaan."

"Yes, this is great," I replied while lowering my gaze from her and in a flat voice.

"But you don't seem happy after listening to this," she said.

"No," I replied smilingly, "I am happy, we will soon be a couple," and in a faint voice I whispered to myself, *"just don't know how these things are happening?"*

"Yup, and bye I have lots of shopping to do, see you," she left.

After some time Aditya came to shop.

"Hey dude what's going," he said.

"Nothing, just time pass over the counter, you say?" I asked.

"So, what happened to your proposal to Anya? you were saying that you will propose Anya soon?" he asked.

"Ya, regarding that, my father asked her father about our marriage, and he said yes and also fixed the date which is next month," I said grimly.

"That's good news bro, so when are you going to become a groom, tell me don't be shy, what's the exact date," he said.

"Ya, I know this is good news, but I am not feeling great. Something is wrong with me or with this world, I feel like a misplaced entity in this world. Everything is strange here. And I am not able to remember many things like when I and Anya became lovers when I decided to sit in this small shop leaving behind my dream of starting a diamond business, and many other things, everything seems odd to me as if I am dreaming." I said with a gloomy look on my face.

"You are thinking too much, just enjoy the life," said Aditya.

"But," as I was about to say further, he interrupted me and said, "no but, just enjoy your life dude, by the way, today evening come to my house I will organise a bachelor party. I will invite all our college friends. Do not be late come at sharp 8 pm, ok I am going I must arrange the party, bye, don't be late."

***

It was 9 pm. The Bachelor party was going on in full swing. I was also having a soft drink along with Aditya. We were sitting on sofas along with other friends.

"You did not tell me when you are going to get married bro?" asked Aditya.

"I already told you that it is next month, why are you asking the same question again and again?" I was a little frustrated at that time. Something was amiss in that scenario. A beautiful girl came near me and sat beside me while touching my soldier lightly with her palm of the right hand,

"Hey handsome, let's have some fun." She said while winking at me. I was visibly at unease at her approach and retraced myself back slightly and asked,

"What do you mean by fun!" I had no clue who she was and why she was behaving like that. Seeing my nervousness Aditya came near me and gently taped my soldier and whispered in my ears,

"Don't worry dude, just have fun. I have arranged her especially for you. After all you are getting married. You will not get such an opportunity ever again".

"What rubbish are you talking about," I shouted as he whispered. Everyone was staring at me.

"It's enough, I am leaving now," said I and left for my home.

After leaving Aditya's home I started on foot toward my home. After a few minutes, Aditya reached me gasping.

"What is this dude, it's your bachelor party and you left. Come on, let's go. I arranged that gal for 5000 bucks." Said he.

"Have I told you to do so?" I replied angrily while still strolling on the footpath.

"I thought it would be a nice surprise for you," he replied.

"I don't like this type of surprise," I said frowningly.

"All right, at least come back to the party".

"I am not interested now, and please don't ask me again."

Now we both were walking on the footpath. It was about 10 pm. Only a few vehicles were visible on the road. After walking for a few minutes, I saw a small handbag beside the road. I picked it up and opened the chain a little to see what it is inside. There was an id and around 10 bundles of notes inside the bag.

"Wow, we got lottery bro. look at these bucks. You are so lucky man," exclaimed Aditya.

"Don't be foolish," I replied, "it's not our money. We must return it to the given address in id".

"You are foolish," shouted Aditya and tried to snatch the bag. I was seeing the greed of money in his eyes.

"Are you out of your mind Aditya, why are you doing this," I shouted angrily.

"Just give me this bag, forget about returning the money. This is my money now." His eyes were red now, which may be due to the consumption of too much alcohol. I pushed him a little bit, he stumbled on the footpath and his head collided with stone and started bleeding. He stood up waveringly somehow. He touched his forehead at looked at his hand. It was covered with his blood now. He became furious at that and picked a small stone and blabbered.

"Give my money or I will kill you,"
Just then our other friends came there and stopped Aditya.

"Take him to his home, he is drunk and blabbering nonsense," I told them and once again marched for my home. I decided to return the money the other day.

***

I ranged the bell. It was the address written on id in the bag. I went there to return the money. A lady, middle-aged opened the door,

"Hello," I said

"Yes," she replied.

"I found this bag on the way to my home last night, I found an id in it, bearing this address so I came to return this bag," I said.

Seeing bag, she exclaimed, "thank god," faintly and tears rolled over her cheeks.

"Please come inside, I am grateful to you for returning this bag," she said.

I entered her home. It was a small house with two rooms and a hall along with one kitchen and one bathroom. I got seated on the sofa as she insisted I sit down. She opened the bag and counted the money. She was relieved to get her money back.

"Please wait while I make a cup of tea for you," said she.

"No need aunty, I have to go now," I said.

"Please wait," she said and went to the kitchen.

After a few minutes I was sipping tea and she was sitting in front of me.

"I am thankful to you, young boy, you returned the money, these days no one returns money just found somewhere on street, I have collected this money for treating my husband. He needs an operation and that require lots of money. Once again, I am thankful to you," she said, and a few drops of tear rolled over her cheeks.

"No need to say thanks over and over, these are after all your money. I just found them, so I returned," I said and finished my cup of tea.

"Ok then I should leave now," while standing up I said.

"Please take some money," she said while giving me some of the money from her bag.

"No need ma'am, these are your money and also you need these for treatment for husband. I have a family business, so I have enough money please don't give me any," I insisted.

Listening to this she smiled and money from her hand disappeared, and sofas also disappeared, everything around us disappeared. It was now a big hall in white colour all around and I was standing there, and she was also standing there having a slight smile over her face. Then she changed her appearance into me as if I was watching a mirror. I was astonished seeing this and was not able to utter a word.

Chapter 12: Kill the Devil

Hero

I gradually regained my memory. I remembered that I had come to the realm of adventure for the test of worthiness and the clone of me standing in front of me was the one, leader of formless creatures of that world.

"Congratulation Ishan you are the first in millennia to pass my test, now drink this," a glass appeared in front of him floating in the air. It was transparent glass having transparent liquid. He said further, "This liquid will help you in awakening your fifth level and also you will know what secret power you will be able to control, don't hesitate just drink this, this is not poison," saying so he smiled sparingly. I drank the liquid inside the glass. After drinking it a strange sensation rushed throughout my body and a colourful light emanated from me, for a few seconds I floated in the air and then landed on the floor. After that everything was normal.

"It seems nothing happed to me there was a colourful show only for a few seconds, so what's my fifth level power once again?" I asked him.

He smiled once again and replied, "don't worry the fifth level secret power takes some time to appear, now as you completed your test it's time for you to leave this realm of adventure," he snapped his finger, and I was enclosed in a transparent bubble.

"I have to ask many things by the way and, also about rocky," before I was able to complete my sentence he said, "you can ask whatever to the sphere of eternity, he will surely reply you," and he pushed me with his palm using telekinesis. Once again I was floating inside a bubble over wast multidimensional space filled with innumerable galaxies.

Within no time I was standing in fifth level class in front of the sphere of eternity.

"Congratulations, it seems you passed the test in the realm of adventure. You can ask anything; I will reply if I know the answer and now you are authorised to hear the answers." Said the sphere of eternity.

"Thanks," I said, "well, I have many questions."

"Shoot your questions. Let me listen to them." Said the sphere.

"First of all, tell me everything about Rocky, how he became black-cloaked devil?" I asked.

"Hmm," voice emanated from the sphere, and it continued, "He was also supposed to be the kind-hearted hero just like you, but he turned to be evil. I don't know, how. His evilness was exposed in the realm of adventure, and he was banished to the dark world."

"But why a good-hearted hero was required? Was there any evil creature just like the black-cloaked guy?" I asked.

"No, there was no evil force at that time. It was my mistake." After saying so sphere remained silent for some time.

"What mistake?" I interrupted its silence.

"Well," sphere started speaking, "I had some error in quantum manipulation of tachyons, you must know about these particles, they are faster than light travelling particles. By studying their behaviour, I was hoping to predict future events. And I was able to see an evil creature coming to this force realm in future and a kind-hearted hero also coming to stop him. So, I asked the king to find the kind-hearted hero and so Rocky was summoned to this world and he became the evil itself. In other words, it is my mistake that resulted in the creation of the cloaked devil. After that, I asked the king to find another kind-hearted hero because only a kind-hearted hero can defeat the cloaked devil. This time also I was sceptical, but you are a kind-hearted hero. I am relieved most."

"So, it's your mess which I am being asked to clean, great," I said in a taunting tone.

"I'm sorry, but you must help this realm. Your fifth level powers will evolve gradually, just wait,"

"I think I need some time to process all these new pieces of information, I will visit you soon. Let me take some rest." I said.

"Very well, I am ready to answer whatever you ask," replied the sphere and I left the hall.

***

As I walked out of fifth level class, around 10 imperial guards encircled me with their swords pointed toward me. One of them came near me, he seemed the leader of this unit and said in a loud voice,

"By the order of her highness, you are hereby arrested for plotting a coup against this kingdom of Endora. Raise your hand in the air or we will have to kill you."

"What rubbish you are talking about." I shouted in anger, "I didn't plot any coup and who is this you're her highness? Is the king no longer the king? Or has he abdicated the crown?"

"You have no right to ask any questions. You are a traitor to this kingdom, and you will be beheaded along with your accomplice Hanna Tucker, just surrender yourself."

It was clear by then that arguing with those people was in vain, so I surrendered myself. I was taken toward the imperial jail inside the king's mansion. I was thrown inside a cell, which was at the third level underground.

It was quite dark inside the cell. I created an illuminating sphere in the air, and it began floating. The cell was engulfed with light now. Hanna was sitting in one corner squeezing her face in between her knees. She looked up and her gaze joined mine. Few drops of tears appeared from her eyes, and she stood up. She came near me running and hugged me and sobbed for a few seconds.

"Where were you Ishan, I was waiting for you, our chief has become queen of this kingdom when the black-cloaked devil kidnapped the king and she accused me of conspiring along with you and no one was telling me where you went," saying so she cried for few seconds and then she wiped her tears. I consoled her by placing my right hand over her head. We both sat there inside the cell.

"What will we do now?" she asked while sobbing.

"I don't know right now, what we should do." I replied, "I have just returned after being tested for fifth level power I need some time to acquaint myself with the current situation and think about any strategy ahead."

"Wow," she was cheerful now, "so tell me did you pass the test and what secret ability you acquired, tell me, tell me." She was excited too.

"Yep, I passed the test," I replied while glancing at her blissful face sparkling as if she had forgotten that we were inside a cell and she was sobbing a while ago.

"I knew you will pass easily now tell me your secret power," she was smiling while saying so. I also smiled in return while glancing at her.

"Oh, come on don't be shy say something." She implored.

"Although I passed I still don't know my secret power yet."

"What," she was shocked hearing this.

"In the realm of adventure, I was tested by formless creatures, and it told me that my secret power will appear gradually over time,"

"Oh, I see, I am sure you will have some cool and awesome secret power," she said.

"I hope so," I replied, and we both smiled.

A few moments of awkward silence followed. I was thinking about my current situation and what to be done now. After a few minutes, she broke the silence.

"I think we should talk the chief; she must be having some confusion that's why she accused us of being conspirators against her,"

"I don't think it would be of any use to talk with chief," I said.

"Why, why are you saying so?" she asked.

"Because the chief is an accomplice of the cloaked devil, she must have asked him to kidnap the king so that she could assume the power," I said.

"What are you saying Ishan? Do you have any proof?" she asked.

"I don't have any proof,"

"Then, how can you say so?'

"King had told me so," I said.

"What! When did king tell you so and why you didn't tell me?" she was a little perplexed.

"When you first time took me to the king, he told me back then and told me not to tell you. I was not sure what to do about that information, so I didn't tell you and I was not sure back then whom to trust,"

"I see," she replied, "that is understandable, after all, you were new here. But what we will do if the chief of the defence department is working with the black-cloaked guy. How we can save the king and this kingdom. I'm not having any idea." She paused for a few minutes.

"I will fight chief and ask her why she did so." I said firmly, "after all I have achieved the fifth level and also, I am the so-called saviour of this kingdom."
She looked at me, her face looked a little disturbed.

"How will you be able to ask her, we are in jail now, are you suggesting jailbreak? We will officially be declared criminal." She said.

"We are already criminal in chief's view, so there is nothing to lose in breaking jail and also I must confront her and have my answers," I said.

"I will help you then," she replied.

"No," I said, "it's going to be a tough task, I don't want to put you in any danger, so you will remain in this jail, and I will go out to find answers,"

"But I want to help you," as she was saying so I enveloped myself with an electromagnetic refractive layer all over my body and became invisible. She was standing there perplexed.

A guard came to see the cell, finding me not in the cell he became hopeless, and a few drops of sweets appeared on his forehead.

"Where is the so-called kind-hearted hero?" he shouted.

"I don't know, he just disappeared," replied Hanna, she was also in shock. Maybe she was pretending to be in shock. Guard went somewhere and after some time a senior officer accompanying him appeared.

"Hanna, tell me, where is the kind-hearted hero."

"I don't know, he just disappeared in front of me. I don't know where he went," replied Hanna. Officer turned his gaze toward the guard and said, "Go inside and search for the kind-hearted hero, he must be hiding somewhere inside, there is no way for him to escape this high-security cell, hurry up."

"Yes sir," said the guard and hurriedly opened the cell. As soon as he opened the gate, I made my escape flying slightly over the floor so that no noise was made.

***

I made myself permeable for the wall and hence entered the king's court. The chief was sitting on the chair of the king. The prime minister, David Hustle was standing in front of him. I was in an invisible state so that they could not see me.

"David hustle, did you find any whereabout of our king, where the black-cloaked devil could be hiding him," asked the chief.

"All the officers of defence department are searching the king but in vain, we are not able to find the king, a few brave officers were close to finding, perhaps the location of the king but they were killed swiftly and easily by someone," after pausing for few seconds he further said,

"Why are we not taking help of Ishaan, after all, he is the kind-hearted hero, why have you put him behind the bar, I couldn't understand why you did this,"

"I did this to save the kingdom of Endora, no one can destroy my kingdom, my motherland, not on my watch, did you understand?" the voice of the chief was furious and loud. Her eyes were blazing red and heated air expulsed through her nostrils.

"I did not get your point, how can putting the kind-hearted behind the bar will help to save our kingdom?" asked the Prime Minister.

"He is not the kind-hearted hero, he is the enemy of the kingdom, the king himself told me," said the chief.

"How can this be possible, he qualified the wishing well test, how can he be not the kind-hearted hero, the king must be having some misunderstanding, I'm sure and also if he is not kind-hearted hero then who will save our kingdom from the black-cloaked devil, tell me," The prime minister was visibly hopeless now.

"I also did not believe whatever the king was saying but then he showed me when so-called kind-hearted hero met the black-cloaked devil and they were planning to kill the king so that they could rule our kingdom together, I saw it myself through my own eyes otherwise I would have never believed. I am sure that Ishan must have helped the black-cloaked devil in kidnapping the king otherwise king would have never lost the fight to the devil, tell me if I am wrong, the devil had never defeated the king before, so tell me how this time he was able to kidnap the king, there can be only one plausible answer and that is, that the so-called hero is not the hero he is traitor to our kingdom, he joined the force with the devil and helped him in kidnapping the king, what do you think now tell me, David, tell me," the chief was furious.

"What you are alleging might be wrong, we must also give Ishan a fair chance to defend himself, don't you think he deserves a chance?" asked the prime minister.

"Absolutely not, he is a traitor and an enemy of the kingdom, he doesn't deserve any chance. He only deserves execution for the crime he has done against the king and the kingdom by becoming an accomplice of the devil. He deserves no mercy. I order his execution immediately. Now pass my order to guard and bring the traitor to me, I will myself execute him." Said the chief.

"But" the prime minister was about to say something as he was interrupted by the chief

"Just follow my order or else you will also be executed along with Ishaan," shouted she.

"As you wish, your highness," he said and left the king's court.

As the prime minister left the court, I encompassed the courtroom with an invisible force field so that no one could enter and disturb my confrontation with the chief.

The chief stood up from the throne as if she was able to feel the force field all around. She shouted,

"Whoever has created this field force just show yourself so that I can decapitate you myself," and a plasma sword appeared in her hand.

I unveiled myself to the chief. Seeing me in front of her she became furious and attacked me with the plasma sword multiple times. I evaded all her strikes floating around her in the air. While attacking me she constructed an illuminating sphere around her left fists and the sphere exploded instantly, it was perhaps some kind of signal to call the guards. Within no time hundreds of guards along with the prime minister appeared outside the court of the king but they were not able to enter the court due to the force barrier enacted by me. They started attacking the force barrier with different types of forces but in vain as my force barrier was of the highest level.

After a few minutes, the chief became tired and backed off a few feet and turned toward the guards and the prime minister and shouted,

"All of you including me had considered this traitor to be a hero but he is no hero, he is also devil because he works with the devil he is his partner in all of his crime, he has helped the devil in kidnapping the king, he must be killed otherwise our kingdom will perish, our king has shown me the true face of him, now I will show his true face to all of you," after saying so, she raised her hand in the air above her, the sphere which was lying beside the throne started floating in the air and a holographic projection appeared in front of it. In the holographic projection, I was seen standing in front of the devil and was seen conversing with him although the voice was not audible and after conversing a few minutes devil hugged me, and the holographic projection ended.

"This is completely fabricated, I never visited the devil," I shouted while looking toward the prime minister who was standing outside the force field.

"He must have forgotten his meeting with the devil," said the chief.

"What do you mean by that, how can I forget it?" I asked.

She once again turned toward the prime minister and said.

"He must have forgotten because when he met with the devil, he was not Ishan, he was also devil,"

"What rubbish you are saying, I am the devil? Are you out of your darn mind, I think after declaring yourself the ruler you have become completely insane, you have become mad," I shouted.

"Ha, ha, ha," now she was laughing, "I think you are losing your sanity to the devil side of yourself"

"Please your highness, spill the bean what do you want to say?" asked the prime minister.

"All right, I will now tell everything in detail," she said, "every human being has two sides, one is the normal side and the other is the devil side. In normal circumstances, normal sides prevail over the consciousness of man and he behaves like a good Samaritan, but when his powers grow the devil side starts to wake up and seeks control over his consciousness and if the devil side wins the person becomes complete devil, just like the blacked cloaked devil. He was also a kind-hearted hero as all of you know, but as he become powerful the dark side of his brain overpowered his good side and he became the black-cloaked devil, the sphere of eternity himself told me so," all the guards started muttering amongst themselves.

"Silent," said the prime minister and all stopped gossiping.

"This is absolutely not true," I said.

"This is true," replied the chief, "maybe your devil side is suppressed right now, but as your devil side has already appeared once, so I can not take any chance. Your devil side will soon consume you completely and you will also become the devil. Before that, I must kill you."

As soon she pronounced so all the guards including the prime minister started shouting

"Kill the devil hero, kill the devil hero, kill the devil hero,"

CHAPTER 13: MERIDOMA: CONTROLLER OF TIME

The chief swung her plasma sword toward me. A beam of high-density plasma leapt toward me. I constructed a force shield in front of me. It was blocking the beam.

"All of you if you want this devil to die lend me your life energy, life energy can pass this barrier," she shouted. All the guards and prime ministers started imparting their life energy into the body of the chief. The intensity of the beam was increasing now. I was being pushed backwards. Within a few `seconds, I collided with the force field which was surrounding the king's court. It was becoming exceedingly hard for me to hold the plasma beam. I was exerting a tremendous amount of force. A few cracks appeared in the shield. I was able to see the death in the form of a plasma beam in front of me. More cracks appeared and the shield shattered along with the force barrier surrounding the court created by me. Within a nanosecond, I was about to be disintegrated into oblivion. Everything seemed to appear in ultra-slow motion then. My whole life till that point of time flashed before my eyes. I thought this was my destiny. To be obliterated into nothingness. I was not able to fulfil my purpose. I was not able to save this realm. I accepted my destiny and closed my eyes.

Nothing happened to me. After waiting a few more seconds, I opened my eyes. I was not inside the king's court. I was inside a transparent oval structure and there were millions of tiny stars floating outside at distance. I was wondering where I had come or how I had come there. Was I dead? Was that heaven or hell? I walked all around, there was no boundary. It seemed infinite oval to me.

A bright light appeared in front of me. A lady appeared with a shining bright gown and a perfectly beautiful face. She was floating in front of me and alighted slowly to my level. She was smiling while looking at me.

"Who are you? Did you bring me here?" I asked.

"I know, you must be having lots of questions, relax I will tell you everything," she said.

"Alright, tell me"

"First of all, I will introduce myself," she said, "I am Meridoma, I am the controller of the flow of time in this realm. I can speed up, slow down or even completely stop the flow of time in the realm of force. I don't have such power in other realms and, I am not God. God has appointed me for this specific purpose only. Although I can alter the flow of time, I can't reverse its flow, in other words I can't go to the past and of course, I can not undo my mistakes. I have strict order not to interfere with whatever going on in the force realm. But I have saved you because only you can undo my mistake."

"What mistake you have done? And do you know me?" I asked.

"Of course I know you," she replied, "I watch everything happening in this realm, only I can't interfere. Last time I interfered, and it resulted in the creation of devil Rocky Bhati, that's why I will help you in defeating him and you will have to help me in undoing my mistake."

"What did you do that resulted in the creation of the devil?"

"In the beginning, there were 18 kingdoms in this realm. Life was running smooth. Everything was perfect. Human being enjoyed their lives and enhanced it with help of lots of their invention. But an aberration in the flow of time occurred which resulted in the appearance of monsters from some other unknown realm. I was desperate in helping human beings, but I was not to interfere with their life. At that time, I had the power of manipulating tachyons and see the future and, I had the power of passing my time controlling abilities to a person having a kind heart. I manipulated the tachyons and created a sphere of eternity so that this sphere could see the future and warn them about upcoming events. I gave this sphere to the kingdom of Elektra; it was one of the nine kingdoms of the dark world. The king of this kingdom seemed kind-hearted to me, so I gave him time-manipulating power. With the help of the sphere of eternity and his power to control the time, the king of this kingdom whose name was Stephon snow, successfully killed all the monsters. After that, for few years prosperity bloomed all over. But I don't know-how, the king became corrupt and power-hungry. He wanted to have more and more power. He asked the sphere, how he can have more power. The sphere told him that there is one another realm, that is your realm, the earth realm from where you have come, there, there is matter called dark matter and it contains one of the deadliest powers of all the realm. So, the king decided to harvest this unknown, so-called most powerful matter. He entered your realm and captured this dark matter and transported it here in compressed form. As soon as he opened it, the dark matter took control over his body, and the dark matter was somehow conscious. It started spreading all over, whatever things came to its contact instantly became dark, whatever people came to its contact became Apators, you must have heard about."

"Yep, I know, one of my friends, unfortunately, was pulled into the dark world and he became Apator, I must find some way to cure him,"

"Oh, that is horrible, because once a person becomes Apator, he can convert back to normal human only if dark matter is defeated, because dark matter sucks the soul and keep it within itself, I don't know why,"

"Then I will defeat this dark matter and save my friend, whether I would die but I will defeat dark matter,"

"I also hope so," said she, "you will have to defeat this dark matter, that's why I saved you. I believe you will help me in defeating dark matter. Although this dark matter is inert in your realm and does not harm your people, but there is a way by which dark matter can gain consciousness in your realm also, and that would be disastrous."

"That is a serious issue, and what happened to the king."

"He was no longer the same king now he was the dark world king. Dark matter was spreading quickly and soon nine kingdoms were its part. I stopped the time and was thinking of some way to stop the dark king. I even thought of fighting him myself, but this was forbidden. I was hopeless. I had stopped the time for a very long time, although no one else in this realm would have perceived that. Then I had an idea. I could stop the time at some localised area in space and hence I created a time stoppage boundary between the dark world and the other nine kingdoms and hence they were saved. But this is a temporary fix and I need some permanent way to defeat the dark king,"

"So, devil not the dark king?" I asked.

"No, he is just one of his puppets from your realm, he has captured many people of your realm who have dark intentions and converted them all into the devil, rocky is not only the black-cloaked devil, but the dark king also has an army of them,"

"Oh my god, so it would be very difficult to defeat them, and also I have not unlocked the fifth level secret power, how would I defeat them,"

"Well, here I'm going to help you,"

"Ok, but how,"

"I will unlock your fifth level power, and this is also one of the reasons why I saved you because you have an affinity to my time power,"

"It means I can also manipulate time like slowing down time?"

"Yes, you can if I unlock it. But if I unlock your power I will no longer exist because only one entity other than God can hold this power and also, I have become bored living so many years now you will have to carry this burden. Despite being able to control the time you will not have the restriction of not interfering with people of this realm so you are more suited to save this realm, finally, I will rest in peace,"

"Oh, I see, so you want to get relieved of your responsibility of saving this world,"

"No, you got me wrong, I don't have such responsibility. I am here to just observe. Because I want to save this world that is why I am transferring my powers to you."

"All right, you did not tell me about the sphere of eternity, how it came to the kingdom of Endora?"

"Well, I don't know many of recent developments, when I erected time stoppage boundary I went into suspended animation, it took me a great time to become conscious again, when I became conscious, I saw you fighting the devil and disappearing to your earth realm accidentally along with Hanna. After that, I observed you closely and find out that you have an affinity to time power and here, we are."

"So, I will have to find answers myself."

"Yep, and also you will have to save this realm, as I have told you after this realm the dark king might attack your earth realm,"

After saying so she closed her eyes and once again started floating above my level. Her whole body started glowing brightly. She was glowing so intensely that I was not able to look at her. I placed the palm of my right hand in front of my eyes. After a few seconds, bright piercing light changed to dim and warm light. I opened my eyes. She was not there. A warm shining sphere was floating in front of me. It was about the size of a football. It came toward me and got absorbed into me. As soon as it got absorbed into me, I was able to see the flow of time all around me. Mysteriously the information about the fifth dimension and time manipulation got embedded into my brain. I was standing in the fifth dimension. All fifth level users had access to the fifth dimension with their personal space there so that no other fifth dimension user could interfere with them in their personal fifth-dimensional space. This space belonged to Meridoma, now it belonged to me.

***

I opened a portal to the cell where I and Hanna were being held. She was happy to see me. She smiled and stood from the floor where she was sitting with a gloomed face.

"I was worried about you, where did they take you?" she asked.

"They took me to the chief, she accused me of conspiring with devil Rocky, somehow I was saved by an angle, Meridoma she took me to her fifth-dimensional space and saved me,"

"Thank god, by the way, who is she? Can I also meet with her?"

"I will tell you everything, but it is not safe here let me take you in my personal fifth-dimensional space, there I will tell you everything,"

I opened a portal to my personal fifth-dimensional space. There I told everything that had happened.

"Oh, so the devil is a mere puppet, the main bad guy is the dark king. Not only he is bad news for this realm he can also attack your realm. Hmmm, this is very bad news. How will we beat him?" she said.

"I am sure I will somehow beat him, after all now I have time controlling power and also I have my personal fifth-dimensional space, if things don't go according to my plan I can always return here and change my strategy," I replied.

"So, what is your strategy?" she asked.

"I will make one soon and of course I will take your help, but first of all, I will have to see the sphere of eternity. I have some questions for him."

"Okey, I will also come with you."

"No, it's risky. Guards of the chief might be waiting for me in the room where the sphere of eternity is placed, it is dangerous. You should wait for me here, I will return soon,"

"No, I will also come with you, I am not weak, I am strong, I will help you in this fight against the dark king,"

"Please, try to understand,"

It seemed futile to argue with her, so I stopped time and made a portal to the room of the fifth level class. I entered the room through the portal. Time was still stopped. The chief was standing in front of the sphere of eternity, maybe she was asking something. I hid under an electromagnetic transparent cloak and started the flow of time.

"Tell me, the sphere of eternity, where is so-called kind-hearted hero hiding. He has betrayed the kingdom of Endora by siding with the devil and helping him kidnapping the king, just use your infinite wisdom and find him so that I could kill him with my hand, just tell me whereabout of him, tell me," said the chief to the sphere, she was visibly furious.

"I am not answerable to you, madam chief. You may have declared yourself the queen, but I don't consider you queen, only a fifth level citizen can be the king, and clearly, you are not the fifth level and, I answer to a fifth level citizen, so I will not answer you anything. You can leave now," said the sphere.

"You are helping a criminal, whether you accept it or not I am the queen now and you must obey my order," said she.

"I am under no obligation to obey your order, I have come to this kingdom under my own free will I am here just to assess the worthiness of fifth level user I do nothing else, did you understood or not, now will you please leave or not," said the sphere.

"You are pathetic useless sphere, just go to hell," shouted the chief and left the room.

"Now, you can unveil yourself, I know you are here, Ishan or the kind-hearted hero," said the sphere. I unveiled myself and confronted the sphere.

"How did you know that I am here," I asked.

"Have you forgotten who am I? I am sphere of eternity, I know everything, only the fifth-dimensional space of the fifth level user, I have no access. I think you met her in her space, tell me what she told you and why she gave her time controlling power to you, I can see the tachyon controlling ability in you, as I can control tachyons, Afterall she made me and gave these powers, now tell me, what happened between you and Meridoma, and what she is planning to stop me?"

"What? Why would Meridoma stop you and from doing what?" I asked while perplexed by sphere's statement.

"It seems that Meridoma has not told you everything or she doesn't know everything, can you tell me what the case is?" asked the sphere.

"Whatever the case may be, you will tell me, just tell me, what you are hiding? If you don't tell me I can use tachyon to trace your past," I told the sphere.

"Be my guest and try that, ha, ha, ha,"

I concentrated tachyons on the sphere to trace its past, but it was resisting. I exerted more and more life energy for the manipulation of after images of residual vibrations so that I could see the sphere's past but all in vain. I was not able to see the past of the sphere. I became frustrated after some time.

"Are you done with your temporal plaything?" said the sphere.

"don't worry sphere, I will soon have my answers and you will tell me," I said.

"that's impossible, well I should tell you. I don't have any offensive powers, but I am foolproof in defence, no one can destroy me. Not even Meridoma, even she had to ask the help of God in stopping me, ha, ha, ha."

"What are you saying?" I murmured as clearly; I was not getting what the sphere was saying.

"All answers need dedication to be found and you think you can just ask everything about me, you are no hero you are a fool. You are one of many fools from the earth realm. It is I who told the chief that you are a kind-hearted hero, but you are no hero, you are one of the ordinary fools of the earth realm. I brought you here so that I could use you in finding a way to dominate all the parallel universe and clearly, I am on right track. Soon I will have all the powers and I will rule on everything for all eternity. I will have complete control over matter and time. I will rewrite the history of every world including your earth realm and in that history, you will be slave of me, a dog of me, ha, ha, ha, you will follow my every order, ha, ha, ha," laughed the sphere. I was becoming restless listening to the sphere's monologue. I decided to destroy the sphere and created a black hole in front of my hand and increased its gravitational field slowly. Sphere floated in the air and started being sucked into the sphere but instead of being frightened, it kept on laughing.

"Ha, ha, ha, you can't even touch me, I have powers of a god. I am the god, ha, ha, ha,"

I intensified the field strength. Suddenly a large number of tachyons appeared all around the sphere and it disappeared in thin air. I closed the black hole and analysed the retracing residual left by the sphere. It appeared that the sphere has fled to its fifth-dimensional space, and I could not follow it. I was hoping that I would get some answers after visiting the sphere but here I had more questions than before? What was the intention of the sphere? Was it the main villain working behind the curtain and controlling all other dark forces? were all other dark forces including the dark king mere puppets of the sphere? What was the role of the sphere in all this mess? My head was exploding inside with all these questions. I remained standing in the room for some time. I somehow gathered my thoughts and decided to visit dark king to have all my answers myself in the dark world. Now I would face the enemy directly.

CHAPTER 14: IS IT THE END?

I opened a portal to my personal fifth-dimensional space. There Hanna was waiting for me,

"don't ever vanish like that ever again, I was so worried about you," she was furious seeing me. I told her everything that transpired in the fifth level class.

"It may be risky visiting dark king, he might be too powerful for you," said Hanna with a concerned look on her face.

"don't worry about me, I now have time controlling power. I can slow down time and even stop time indefinitely. If anything goes wrong in the dark world, I will simply stop time and escape here in my fifth-dimensional space, no one except me can enter here and of course, with my permission they can enter here." I spoke.

"But I'm not feeling well about this, you must take extra precaution there and do come back, promise me," she said.

"I promise, I will come back, but first I will drop you in your home, your mother must be worrying about you," I said.

"Okay," was her reply.

I opened a portal to her house. We descended into the dining hall of her house. Her mother was sitting on the sofa and watching television. Seeing her, her mother slowly stood, and tears flowed over her cheeks. They both hugged.

"I was worried about you, I heard those guards of defence department arrested you, I went there, they were not telling me anything about you, I was..." her mother was sobbing while saying so.

"It's all right now, I have come. Ishan helped me," said Hanna.

"Thank you, son," said her mother, "take a seat, I will immediately make tea for both of you, just wait," and she hurried toward the kitchen. I looked at Hanna, she smiled.

"I have to go now; I can't waste any time. Dark king might be planning to attack this kingdom or my realm, no one is safe now. Destiny of all multiverse lies upon my soldiers, and I don't know whether I would be able to fulfil my destiny or not,"

She glanced at me, "You will surely fulfil your destiny. I have complete faith in you. Take care and do come back," a few tears rolled over her cheeks. I wiped her tears,

"I'll be back," I said.

I opened the portal and entered into my personal fifth-dimensional space. From there I opened another portal and went near the boundary of the dark world. Within the boundary, time was still. I was able to see all the mythical ancient creatures frozen in space-time within the boundary indicating that it was created by Meridoma, aeons before the present time. I tried to open a portal for the other side of the boundary, but it did not work out. Perhaps to enter into the dark world there was no shortcut, I had to cross the boundary. As I started my flight to enter into the boundary Meridoma appeared in front of me,

"Stop, don't enter into boundary otherwise you will also get trapped in it. Nothing can escape this boundary."

I was surprised at her being alive,

"You are alive, but I saw you disappearing into oblivion," I asked.

"I am not Meridoma, I am only after the image of her she created me while being obliterated so that I can stop you when you take any rash decision,"

"If I cannot cross this boundary, how will I be able to defeat the dark king? Tell me?" I asked.

"There is only one way," she said.

"Tell me,"

"But this will result in permanent disappearance of me. I am made by special tachyon, and only the person possessing this tachyon can cross this time stoppage boundary, any other entity if tries to cross this boundary would be trapped into it indefinitely,"

"There must be some other way, I need your guidance in defeating dark king,"

"There is no other way, this is the only way. I will have to transfer my special tachyons to you so that you could cross the boundary, its ok, after all, I am only after image, I am not real Meridoma," she was smiling while saying so and I was feeling uneasiness. She was ready to sacrifice herself that show the amount of trust she had in me.

"There must be some other way," I insisted but she smiled, and some sparkling particles emitted from her and entered into my body. Soon she once again disappeared in front of me, while being disappeared she said,

"Please save this world,"

These words echoed in my ears. Within no time all particles got absorbed into me. I felt more connected to the time stream flowing through space. I was able to distinguish between time and space itself. Perhaps Meridoma gave all her power to me.

Within no time I crossed the boundary. Dark forces were not able to affect me perhaps due to powers given to me by Meridoma, she died so that I could have such powers. She had burdened me with the task of saving this realm and all other realms. As soon as I entered the dark world a strange creature appeared in front of me. It had the body of a human but the head of some mythical dragon. It also had thrones on its head,

"Ha, ha, ha, welcome Hero, dark king welcomes you in his kingdom,"
He said with his deep voice, he was floating, and dark matter was enveloped all over his body like a flame.

"Who are you?" I asked.
Sphere of eternity appeared there, and voice emerged from it,

"You insolent fool. How dare you ask a question to the Greatest king of all multiverses, the dark king. He will soon conquer this realm and after that, he will conquer the earth realm of yours, you should be trembling in front of his majestic appearance, you are nothing in front of him. You are just a small pebble to be crushed by him,"

"Well," I said, "so he is so-called dark king, now I will not have to search for him. He has made my task easy by coming to me himself, after finishing him I will finish you also,"

"What… are you out of your mind, you will finish the dark king, ha, ha, ha, clearly you don't know anything about this dark world. In this dark world he is God, he is the creator of this dark world, and every rule of this dark world is made by him, you have done a huge mistake by entering this world, no one can help you now," said the sphere.

"We will see," I said.

"Ha, Ha, Ha," laughed the dark king, "I think you are not understanding your position here. You are nothing here. You can do nothing here. I am the god of this world, real god not some fake god, like Meridoma."

"Really… you are a god?" I asked.

"If you have doubt, you can do anything, attack me with all yours might, you can't even put a scratch on me here, just try and fulfil your amusement because after that I will kill you,"

I became a little worried listening to his claim. Nevertheless, I collected some of my life energy within me and amplified it with tachyons provided by Meridoma, a shining shield-like layer appeared all over my body. I concentrated energy on my palm and fired energy balls toward the dark king with my right hand and toward the sphere with my left hand. The dark king made some gestures with his hand and a shield appeared in front of him, made of dark forces, energy balls collided with the shield generating tremendous fireworks and sparkles and it pushed him backwards. On the other hand, the sphere once again disappeared.

"Such a weak life force," grinned the king and a dark spear appeared in his other hand, and he launched it toward me. I contrived a shield in front of me, the spear collided with the shield pushed me several feet backwards. Dark rays emanated at the point of collision. Within a few seconds, cracks started to appear in the shield and it shattered into pieces. The spear was about to pierce my chest but a few nanoseconds before that I stopped the time and drifted aside, out of the line of attack of spear and started time once again. The spear went along with its trajectory and pierced into the boundary where it became stationary. My eyesight now drifted toward the king. He had created a gun like structure in his hand and started firing at me. I flew all around while evading dark bullets coming from his dark gun and counter-attacking with my balls of energy. After a few minutes, he stopped firing and I descended on the ground a few feet away from him.

"You can do nothing here, your time controlling gimmick is useless here. Even with stopping time you can not even touch me," he grinned once again. I was becoming frustrated. I collected high voltage electricity on my hand and thrusted it toward the dark king, once again it collided with the dark shield with no effect. I constructed a tiny black hole and launched it toward him, and it simply got absorbed into him.

"Ha, Ha, Ha, a black hole is an extension of dark power, it will be simply got absorbed by me, now playtime over," after saying so a fine quality sword made of pure diamond appeared in his hand. I recognised it. It was the sword of king Justin Edgar.

"That is the sword of king Justin Edgar, how did you get it? Did you kidnap the king, tell me what you did with him?" I asked loudly.

"You can have all your answers from your god, whose power has no consequence in this dark world, here I am the god," after saying so the dark king vanished in thin air and appeared just a few inches ahead of me, swung his sword at my throat. He was too fast for me to follow, somehow, I stopped time and the sword was just one inch away from my throat. Time stoppage tachyon filled all over me and the dark king. Space-time started vibrating all around me. I took a few steps away from the dark king. The time was stopped but his dark energy was piercing the stopped space-time continuum. Soon he was able to move his body within the stopped time framework. I was stunned seeing this. How he was able to do this. I became anxious. Since he can now freely move within the stopped time then he can also cross the time stoppage boundary. I had to stop him now. The dark king looked toward me and laughed,

"I did tell you that I am god, here," after saying so he flew toward me. Although he was able to resist my time stoppage field, his speed was average in my time stoppage field. I drifted toward the side, as he swung the sword, which I evaded easily. His body momentum pushed him toward the boundary, but he inserted the sword in the ground stopping him from entering the boundary. He barely touched the boundary. Maybe he was still frightened by it or maybe he can resist the time stoppage field of mine but not that of the boundary. He looked toward me.

"Still afraid of boundary, clearly you are not a god," I mocked him.

He looked at me and grinned, he swung his sword over his head and dark force from all around started collecting there, a cyclone of dark force appeared over his head and everything all around him started being sucked into it. My body also flew into the air and started going toward it. I used all my life energy to stop myself but in vain. I was slowly being pulled toward the cyclone.

"Now it is your time to die, don't be upset, it is your fortune that you are being killed by a god," he laughed after saying so. I was fully invested in stopping my self being sucked into the dark cyclone that I did not realise that the sphere of eternity appeared just beside me.

It started sucking the special tachyon from me given by Meridoma. I was once again seeing the end of me. At one end I was being sucked into the dark cyclone and on the other hand, my special tachyon which was saving me from dark energy was being sucked away by the sphere of eternity, the sphere of eternity was also unaffected by the time stoppage field of mine. Was this the end of me? it might be true after all that I am not a hero.

"This is your end, so-called fake kind-hearted hero, you will die now," said the sphere, "the dark king was waiting for this special tachyon for aeons, and you fool delivered it to him, ha, ha, ha. With the help of this tachyon, anyone can cross the boundary created by Meridoma and soon after crossing the boundary the whole of nine other kingdoms will bow to the dark king and after that, he will enter your earth realm and destroy it completely. You have given enough headache to him. he will not conquer your world. He will destroy your world and you will be the reason for its destruction. Ha, ha, ha, it was your ultimate mistake to come here. Now you can only grieve for a few more seconds as you are about to die," the sphere was engaged in monologue and only one

thought crossed my brain,

"Is it the End?"

Chapter 15: Trapped for Eternity

Just then I opened a portal to my fifth-dimensional space between me and the dark cyclone and eased out the resisting force against the cyclone. I was immediately pulled toward the portal and entered into my fifth-dimensional space and the portal closed. I checked the amount of special tachyon on me, luckily it was reduced by less than one percent only, so the other side of the boundary was still safe from the dark king. Now I understood that only this special tachyon is the thing that is needed by the dark king to conquer or destroy the force realm. Only after getting this special tachyon, he can cross the time stoppage boundary. In other words, if I destroy this tachyon, he will not be able to do any harm to this world and my world also. I remembered that the tachyons are faster than the speed of light particles, if somehow, I will be able to slow down the speed of tachyons below the speed of light then it will automatically get destroyed. I started collecting all special tachyon over my palm and applied anti tachyon field over it, but I was disturbed by the voice of the sphere,

"What are you doing so-called kind-hearted hero?"

I got disturbed and special tachyon got stretched all over my body once again. I turned and it was the sphere along with the dark king in my fifth-dimensional space. I was deeply shocked because it was not possible to enter others fifth-dimensional space but here, they had entered.

"You seem confused," said the sphere "seeing us here."

"But how is this possible? How both of you entered into my fifth-dimensional space?" I asked.

"No more questions," said the dark king and once again raised his diamond sword above his head and swirled it heavily but there was no dark cyclone, seeing that I smiled and immediately applied the time stoppage force field and all the motion of the dark king ceased. Maybe because he had no extra dark energy to help him there. The sphere was not affected by time stoppage force, but it was of no immediate concern as he had no offensive ability.

"Now, both of you did a mistake this time. In this dimension, I can stop time indefinitely, in other words, I have defeated your dark king, and," after saying so I sucked the little amount of special tachyon from the sphere and the dark king that the sphere has taken from me, "I take back my special tachyon," while saying so.

"No," was the response of the sphere which indicated that I had hit the jackpot.

"Now," I said, "Tell me how you and dark king were able to enter into my fifth-dimensional space, you have all the time here, as time is stopped and also you can not escape from here and also your dark king can not escape, so it would be better for you to just answer my question."

"You are mistaken in considering this fifth dimension as yours," the sphere replied.

"What!" I said and clearly observed the fabrication of space, and it became clear now, it was the fifth-dimensional space of Meridoma. In haste, I had opened the portal to her space.

"That doesn't explain how you and the dark king came here?" I asked.

"Well," replied the sphere, "I had some of your special tachyon and half of that tachyon I gave to the dark king, and it acted as a key to enter into this space,"

"And now both of you are trapped forever here as I will destroy all special tachyon and after that, both of you will be trapped here forever," after saying so I collected all the special tachyon on my palm and applied speed slowing anti tachyon on it, within few seconds all the special tachyon disappeared.

"What have you done? You are out of your mind," shouted the sphere "you will also get trapped here, along with us for eternity,"

"That is not going to happen," I said, "Meridoma has given this space to me, I can exit and enter here without the help of the special tachyon. Now I am leaving, and both of you do enjoy your eternal prison here since both of you are trapped for eternity here. bye, bye,"

I said and opened the portal to the dark world near the boundary.

When I arrived at the dark world, it was no longer a dark world. Dark energy was leaving. The time stoppage boundary had also disappeared. Flora appeared all around as if this land was free from the curse of darkness. I used my electromagnetic search power and find out the location of Aditya, it seemed that he was no longer an Apator now. He has become normal. I went near Aditya flying. He was extremely happy and astonished to see me.

"Hi, Ishaan, do you know what place is this, it seems like a fairy kingdom. They're so colourful flora all around, and I don't remember how I came here." He spoke. I went near him and hugged him.

"Hey, Ishaan, are you alright? You seem emotional?"

"Nah, I am alright," I said, "just seeing you after a long time,"

"What are you saying, we are meeting after a long time?"

"Yep,"

"I did not get," he replied.

"Well, tell me what the last thing you remember," I asked. He tried to remember his last memory and said,

"You and I were inside the mine of Rocky Bhati, I think, there was a strange well from which diamonds were coming out flying and we were caught, and I think I jumped into that well, oh my god, I remember nothing after that and when I got awakened, I was here, do you know what happened," he asked.

I told him everything that had happened after that he was completely shocked listening to me and laughed also,

"So, you are saying that you are a hero of this force realm," he said mockingly.

"Yep, that is what I am here," I replied while grinning.

"How did I become normal after becoming Apator? Can you explain that?" he asked.

"I don't know, maybe because dark king got trapped into fifth-dimensional space of Meridoma that's why dark energy got weakened and left this place and also the hold of dark energy got weakened on you that's

why maybe your astral body got united with your physical

body, this is only my hypothesis. I am not sure about it." I

spoke.

"And you are right," a voice appeared from

behind. This was the voice of Rocky Bhati, I turned

toward him.

"don't come near us," I warned.

"don't worry," he said, "I am no longer black-

cloaked devil, in fact, I never was the black-cloaked devil

in the first place,"

"What are you saying?" I asked, "if you were not

a black-cloaked devil then who was he? Don't say that he

was your twin brother who got lost in the fair of Kumbh,"

I grinned. Aditya also laughed. Rocky Bhati also

chuckled listening so and he said,

"Well, I am the real king of the Kingdom of

Endora," as soon as he said so I became shocked.

"What, clearly you are lying. You are not king, I

know the name of the king, he is Justin Edgar, and you

are not Justin Edgar," I said firmly. Rocky smiled and spoke.

"I know I am not Justin Edgar; I am Rocky Bhati, and I am the real king of the Kingdom of Endora,"

"How is this possible," I asked.

"Will you allow me to say my side of the story," he said annoyingly.

"Ok, say your side of the story," I said.

"Very well," he said, "I am Rocky Bhati, once again, and I am the king of the kingdom of Endora, although I am not from Endora. I am from earth. I was bestowed the title of king by the previous king of the Kingdom of Endora whose name was Robert Hill, he had no offspring so he built the wishing well so that worthy candidates from other worlds could pass through it and become the next king, and by an accident, I fell into the well and came here. I got selected as the next king and got trained as a king. They had a test after which I was selected as king. I passed the test the same way you passed it. In other words, I appoint you the next king of the kingdom of Endora, congratulations, now you will think why this test was necessary? This test was necessary because as a king you will get such powers by which you can see the whole history of this world and many other capabilities, you will get all the answers of your all questions so don't worry about it and when the time would be right you will also select someone else to replace you,"

"What are you saying, I just can't get it," I said.

"don't worry, when I will pass the eternal power of the king to you, you will get all your answers," after saying so he closed his eyes and his whole body got converted into a sphere of light and it got absorbed into my body, it was eternal power, and only after the destruction of the whole body of carrier of this power, it could be transferred into other body. Within a few seconds after getting eternal power I had all my answers, I looked toward Aditya and said,

"Now, I know everything,"

"Tell me," He asked.

"Whatever happened, to me or you were nothing but deep sleep ramification created by Rocky Bhati using eternal power so that he could test my eligibility to be next king of the kingdom of Endora, although it happened in the real world. Some of its characters were real and some were simply guided by eternal power. The dark king was real and also meridom was real. All other characters behaved the way they were behaving only to test me and also unconsciously. that's it, nothing else."

I teleported Aditya to the earth realm where he wrote my story.

THE END